THE PROUD GUNS OF THOMPUS TOWN

THE GREAT WESTERN SAGA

CHESTER W. MCNEAL

authorHOUSE®

AuthorHouse™
1663 Liberty Drive
Bloomington, IN 47403
www.authorhouse.com
Phone: 833-262-8899

Published by AuthorHouse 08/31/2022

ISBN: 978-1-6655-6843-2 (sc)
ISBN: 978-1-6655-6848-7 (hc)
ISBN: 978-1-6655-6849-4 (e)

Library of Congress Control Number: 2022915188

Print information available on the last page.

If one happens to be a jack - rabbit or a roving a coyote crossing the prairie on this particular fast night, one might catch the flickering flames of a lone cowpoke's campfire. Naaman Rum, discontented drover, got himself fired from a cattle drive, was making his way back home when stopped for the night to rest his horse as well as himself for the ride over the western plain had been long. Rolling up his sleeves, he took his bedroll from his saddle, and bed down for the night.

Eyes heavy with sleep, Rum almost fails to hear the whining of his horse. He awakes momentarily, but being as tired as he was, he drops back off to sleep only to be awakened again by something bumping against his boot. He opens his eyes to see the figure of a man standing at his feet. " Who - who are ye? " Rum asked nervously.

"What do ya want?"

"Easy, stranger," the man answered. "I'm Kirby Carson, deputy sheriff. I just want to share your campfire." Rising from his stooping position, Carson began to unsaddle his horse.

Naaman Rum sits up to take in all that is going on, "I was a drover," he said, "driving cattle for what seems to be a life - time. I got disgusted and practically quit the job.... Well, er, the trail-boss fired me. I was heading for Gun-Fire Valley and await my pay."

"Gun-Fire Valley, eh?"

"That's where I law at. I'm returnin' to town from deliverin ' a prisoner to the big jail at the county, " Carson said.

⚭

A big man known as 'King Thompus' sitting in a high place in the prison - yard surrounded by interested listeners as he tells how he organized three lawless towns outlaw haven for men on the dodge and how he ran each town as their outlaw chief and Kingpin.

Interesting enough is how the town of Delton got its name more accidental than anything else, it was named for a ruthless outlaw. Thompus, a burly man standing over six feet tall, with brownish, gray hair, got acquainted with Rinald Delton, the gun fighter, when Delton walked nervously into the saloon established by Thompus.

The town was unnamed and underdeveloped with less than a dozen houses, some half- finished, buildings under construction, cabins, farms, homesteaders and growing. The men wore their six - shooters, but few of them were considered gunmen, so Delton had nothing to fear from the townspeople. He was tired of running and camping out and now he could rest. Nevertheless, he was constantly on his guard. Realizing he had nothing to fear, he bullied his way into owning the town. With no laws and no challenges, Delton had his way in this area. Thompus had no quarrel with the gunfighter, but he was not comfortable with him around. However, it gave him an idea that would expand his territory. The taxes he levied on homesteaders and farmers along with his own special rules and regulations enabled him to expand. To pacify the men who seemed to rule their contentment, the people donated live stocks and community service to help further establish Thompus' domain. He became known to them as 'King Thompus the Hat' for he loved to wear enormous hats as he would ride proudly among those that held him in high esteem.

Thompus had become wealthy in Arizona where he was in business with his sister's husband, Clifford Porter. Porter died leaving five sons and a stepdaughter. The business was failing as Thompus sold it to a new firm. Thompus took his fortunes and reestablished himself in Texas. He set up a saloon in a large vacant area and began to build a town where homesteaders were rapidly settling. Outlaws on the run began to find safe haven in the new area. Thompus had influential friends like Benjamin Masters and a retired Calvary Colonel name Richmond Epps working with him and together they had their circle of henchmen They had seniority over any group of outlaws and let them know that living here would cost a sizeable fee. Outlaws, tired of running, obliged, however, Rinald Delton was an exception.

Now, Thompus' plan was to establish a town three miles west where a valley lay below two mountain ranges. He had gotten acquainted with the Indian tribes that lived on each mountain range. Chief Montus-known as 'Big Mountain' and his tribe was on one side and a younger chief name 'Flaming Eagle' and his tribe was on the other side. Below were grasslands for cattle with room on the other side for sheep. Thompus showed his friends how fast the first town had grown. The new one would grow just as fast. The wide creek that watered the wild horses would be plentiful enough for all.

"That's where we need to establish," Thompus told his men.

"I know that area," the Colonel said. "It's fertile, all right, but you are forgetting one thing."

"Yeah," added Masters, "The Indians."

"Let me tell you about the Indians," Thompus said.

As Angus Thompus began to tell his friends how he had befriended the Indians, his mind ran back to his plan for settling the new valley. His sister had passed away and he was sending for his five nephews and their stepsister. Thompus was thinking that if one lawless gunfighter could have a town in terror just by living there, he could send for his 'guns', five nephews and their stepsister, but he wanted to settle a new area for them to move to.

Anytime the original town was mentioned, Delton's name would come up. Delton's name would come up often that some people thought that was the town's name. One person called the town 'Delton' by mistake and everyone else began to call the town 'Delton'. Rinald Delton was not aware of this. The people in and around the town literally thought that was the name—and so it was.

Thompus, however, settled another town three miles from Delton before the Porters arrived and that is the town, they settled in.

Meanwhile, the way Gun-Fire Valley was settled all came from the plan of Angus Thompus to not have to be anywhere near the know gunman,

Rinald Delton. Now, as he tells the Colonel and Ben Masters how he met the Indians of the mountain ranges, he began to say, "I once rescued a young Indian boy from a bear," said Thompus.

"His father was not close enough to help, but he saw my heroic deed and took me back to his trailer."

"I suppose they made you a blood-brother, eh?" asked Ben.

"Naw but close. When I got to the Indian camp, the chief and some braves and an old white man who was blood- brother to the chief met me. I was accepted into the tribe gladly. Now, whenever a wagon scout, or wagon train, or any white man that wants a safe passage thru Indian territory, all they have to do is call out 'THE HAT! King Thompus the Hat!' And the Indians—even some of the renegade Indians—will let them thru."

"That's quite a story, Thompus," said the Colonel. "I'm quite familiar with it. I just needed to know that meant for ALL the tribes.

"Anyway," Thompus went on ignoring Colonel, "there's room on each range for cattlemen as well as the much-hated sheep men. We get ourselves established as a town between those two mountain ranges, we can collect from the sheepmen and the cattlemen. It won't take us long to get a settlement going. Then, I'll send for my nephews and all and we WILL rule."

"What's wrong with doing all that here?" Asked Ben. "The town is practically built. Does Delton rattle your chain that much?"

"We'll let Delton have this place," Thompus said, "the place I'm talking about holds much more promise—grazing land and such."

So, taking his carpenters, blacksmiths, and builders, King Thompus, the Colonel, And Ben masters went to work and soon wagon trains were bringing in new settlers and the new town called 'Gun-Fire Valley' was established. To assure that there was some kind of law, Ben Masters was appointment Sheriff.

As the new town continued to grow, a saloon, a bank, a school, and a church was also established. Meanwhile, King Thompus kept things going and growing.

In his first town and when someone would refer to the first town, Thompus would say "Delton! He's still there. I am yet in control all right, but Delton!! He makes me nervous." When the people would hear Thompus say anything pertaining to the first town, all they really hear was 'Delton!' So, some of them assumed that was the name of the town. Even when the town continue to grow, it was still referred to as Delton. Even when Rinald Delton decided to move on, not even knowing the town was called after his name, it was still referred to as Delton so thus Delton became the town's official name.

When the Porter brothers and their sister moved from Arizona to Gun-Fire Valley as their uncle Thompus had requested, they practiced they're gun play and would put on exhibitions of entertainment to show off their firearm skills.

Later on, some of King Thompus' connections informed him that a miner was seeking gold about three miles from Gun-Fire Valley and discovered a silver mine. Thompus immediately got his Indian connections to frighten the miner into selling his findings, so King Thompus began developing the town of Gun-Belt in that area. The silver mine soon ran its short-lived course, but a new town—a third town was established under King Thompus the Hat.

He employed a gambler known as Johnny 'Sweet-Shot' Logan to run the saloons in Gun-Fire Valley and GunBelt. A smooth businessman name 'Lee Venon Rose' was selected to run things in all three towns assisting Thompus. He soon became mayor of Gun-Fire Valley with henchmen in Delton and GunBelt. Thompus decided to have his sister, his niece, and his five nephews settle in GunBelt so that his business partners and associates wouldn't know he every move, but his sister died.

Johnny 'Sweetshot' Logan later moved his activities to Delton. His connections with various gunmen would assure him of no *problems with the return of Rinald Delton.*

When Johnny 'Sweetshot' Logan was being hassled by Sheriff Ben Masters for his unscrupulous dealings as Gun-Fire Valley's Saloon chief, Logan thought it best to move his activity to the town of Delton. With co-operation and assistance from King Thompus, he moved on. With Logan's connections with other gunman from various states, he convinced them to come to Delton.

Some of these men had cause to hate Rinald Delton so this move pleased Thompus. When Delton realized he may have had trouble on his hands, he decided to move on. L. Venon Rose then moved his office to Delton.

Rinald Delton, as a young man, was hailed as a hero in Colorado, but things changed, and certain events put him on the wrong side of the law. Innocent as he may have been in most of the circumstances that confronted him as a young gunman, one of his bullets hit a deputy sheriff. To escape the hangman's noose, Rinald Delton was on the run. Now, he was to move on from a town called by his name to a more peaceful environment. As he saddled his mount, he recalled how one challenge after another had caused a number of men to fall by his gun. Now at Delton, he had had peace but now he knew it would be short-lived…so on his rode to an uncertain destiny.

While that was happening, King Thompus was continuing to prosper in Gun-Fire Valley, however, his biggest problem was the sheriff he had appointed. Ben Master was a man of scruples and believed in doing things the right way. When Thompus would send men to do a certain job, Ben Masters would step in and foil the plan going so far as to arrest some of Thompus' men.

Since Ben Masters and King Thompus were friends as well as partners in their ventures, Thompus had to be careful on how he was to handle this situation without changing their relationship. So, using his connections and influences certain government officials, he got Ben Masters promoted to U.S. Marshall and had him moved to a much larger town in Colorado. A young deputy was appointed to hold the position of sheriff until the office was to be properly filled. Kirby Carson, a tall, dark-haired gunman fit the bill as deputy. He had reached the job as deputy when the sheriff had formed a posse to round up three brothers who were on the run after a shootout that they had instigated.

Ben Masters suspected that his friend King Thompus had made his promotion arrangements, but he gladly went along with the move. Masters felt bad that he could not prevent Thompus from running guns to his Indians Tribe connections and when the whiskey wagons roll in from Philadelphia and let the Indians know, after his saloons had their appropriate amount.

"My good friend Angus the Hat!" griped Ben to Colonel. "That wagon load of rifles that the army missed, he can account for. I can't prove it, but you know him, Colonel! You know him as well as I do."

"Well, Ben, I guess we both closed our eyes to many times while Angus operated. His big mistake was to make you Sheriff. Well, it's no longer your problem. I'm cutting loose from him myself. My horse ranch is well established. My farm is going to keep me and my men quite busy on the outskirts of town. Whatever he and his hired hand do within that town is completely on him now. He won't listen to either one of us anymore. He's out of control. 'King Angus Thompus the Hat'! Well!"

"My money will be made honestly from here on out, I tell you. This new Marshall job will keep me clear of Thompus Towns," Ben said to the Colonel. "So long, buddy. Take care."

"You, too, Ben. Keep in touch when you can. We accomplished a lot, we did." said the Colonel as Ben rode off.

Kirby Carson inherited the sheriff job in the lawless town of Gun-Fire Valley. People wondered if he would follow the law as Ben Masters who so set the example, or would he follow King Thompus the Hat style of order? Carson had his own agenda. There was a particular case when a man behind bars seem to not belong there, and Carson's way of looking at it was interesting.

Mysteriously, a prisoner escaped. The deputy was getting up off the floor, holding his head when the people came into the jail. It was said that a man draped in a black robe, or cloak had entered the jail, downed the deputy, and released a prisoner. After a few more incidents of this same order, the people began to think there was no such mystery rider releasing various prisoners and fix their eyes on Carson himself.

As the night faded into morning, Naaman Rum and Kirby Carson saddled their horses and headed for the town of Gun-Fire Valley. As they near the border, Rum turned his mount and said to Carson,

"I'm going to run by the farm before I go into town."

"What for?" As Carson as he stopped his horse.

"The big farm I once owned. I still got my folks running it, but I don't own it anymore."

"You mean the Colonel's farm right next to... next to his horse ranch? I know that place. How'd you lose it?"

"Gambling, dag-nab it! I shot the whole farm to that so-called King Thompus! I'd like to...dag -nab it! I gotta go by there."

"How did the Colonel get it from Thompus? And while he owns it, why is your family still there?" Carson hesitated and then exclaimed. Rum! Naaman Rum! I didn't make the connection when you told me your name. The 'Rum' Farm. Huh!"

"Well, you know the Colonel and Thompus are in this partner-thing together, but the Colonel is a straight up guy. They're as different as night and day. Anyways, the Colonel knew of my family status and the hard work we've done to get that farm together, so he talked Thompus in to letting him have the farm since it is so close to his horse ranch. Thompus agreed on some kind of settlement, but he wasn't gonna just give it to the Colonel, so he allowed my family to stay there and run the place. I just couldn't stay. I was too ashamed. I joined a cattle drive and stuck with that kind of work for a while, but I check in every now and then on the place and on my family."

"Yeah," said Carson, "I met your folks. I was in a posse. We were running down some outlaws Sheriff Bands had been tracking, Bands had formed a posse, deputizing each man in it. On the road, my horse stepped in a gopher hole and almost broke his leg. He was lucky, but I wasn't. The horse fell on my left leg, but not with all his weight, but it did put me out of commission for a spell. Some of the men took me to the nearest place to get me some help.

That place was the Rum Farm. The bunkhouse where all the men that runs the Colonel's horse-ranch was full, so they put me up at the farmhouse to mend.

The doc would come out from town to help me mend. Life was swell. I'm living on a farm; I would say when I wrote to my brothers. Sunny and Bill used to be out here in the west, but the east-wind blew them in another direction."

"Women?" Asked Rum.

"Yeah," he said Carson. "Linda and Alice."

As Carson and Rum rode by the bunkhouse where farm hands and ranch hands would sleep, they a far were greeted by a young lady and a beautiful black stallion.

"Whoa, Night," said she pulls on the stallion reigns.

"Hi," she said to the riders.

"Hello there," Carson answered "you're quite a rider. I know one when I see one."

"Yeah," added Rum. "Every Fourth of July, my horse out runs every horse in the yearly race. You and that animal are sure prize winners."

"Why aren't you in town, Mr. Lawman? Are you aware the bank robbery last night?" asked the young lady.

"Bank robbery? I'd better get to Gun-Fire Valley let's split!" exclaimed Carson. "I'll be back later." And he was off in a haste.

"Mr. Rum, I haven't seen you for a while," the young lady said. "I'm sure your family will jump for joy when they see you."

"Yeah, I'm sure." answered Rum.

"Where did you run into Kirby?" She asked.

"Back on the dusty trail," answered Rum. "He woke me from a deep sleep back on the prairie. I couldn't share any beans or coffee with him... I ate 'em all up. Didn't have that much anyways. You wanna to ride with me to see my folks?"

"Why not? Midnight will be ok while I greet your folks."

"Midnight? I heard you call him 'Night', I reckon that's short for Midnight," said Rum.

"Right," said the young lady as they dismounted and headed for the farmhouse.

As Kirby Carson entered Gun-Fire Valley, a crowd of townspeople met him. "The bank!" they cried, "the bank has been robbed! Somebody knew you were out of town. They knew it! That's why this town needs more than a deputy!"

"Now, just hold it," Carson said to the excited crowd. "What time did all this take place?"

As Carson selected certain men from the crowd, they settled down in the sheriff's office to discuss the details of the event that took place during his absence.

"I'm thinking that between these three-gun towns 3 to 5 miles apart, somebody knew the sheep men's payroll was in the bank. I've got some investigating to do," Carson said to the group.

"Well, you can start with the Sherley brothers," said one of the men.

"They've been harassing some of the townsfolk anyway they can."

"Maybe," said Carson "but are they bank robbers?"

"Well, it's a wide range to check out. Everybody knows the cattlemen get paid one week and the sheepmen get paid the following week. There is always trouble when they come to town and confront each other." another man said.

"What's that got to do with the problem at hand?" ask Carson.

"Let me handle this."

Back at the Rum farm, Naaman is conversing with his sons and their young wives, while his wife is making bread. The young lady listened with much interest. Naaman was telling his listeners more concerning the three towns organized by King Thompus the Hat.

"One thing special about Thompus," he said, "even though he established saloons in each town, and a bank, a school, and what we call the hot house where a fella kin find certain flashy women, (ha ha) Well, anyway, Thompus always sees that a church is built and it's kind of funny, the kind of man he is, and he never misses a church service on Sunday and he makes all the Bible classes. That seems a little strange to me. This guy beat me out of this farm and… Well, anyway…"

"Maybe he feels somewhat guilty," the young lady stated.

"Well, maybe," said Rum "I guess he is put away for a while. I got that news while I was on the cattle-drive to Colorado a couple of years ago. I never heard what they finally got him on. I guess I was too busy being a driver I missed out on a lot. How can any normal man win in a card game with men like 'Three Queens' Denny and Sweetshot Logan running the deck? I guess I never should've sat in with those shifty guys."

"By the way, girly…you're the Colonel's daughter, aren't you?" Rum asked the young lady.

"Yes, I mean … yes, I ' m his adopted daughter. My name is Shelley Weston, I guess I ' m the only one ever hear my dad call King Thompus by his real name."

"Angus is it?" asked Rum.

"Angus Preston Thompus," answered Shelley.

"Yeah! And because he ruled with an iron fist," Rum added, "He declared himself a king. I gotta give the man his dues. He used every angle at his disposal and even those that weren't. He's a self - made champion."

"Love him or hate him, I guess be earned his title." Shelley added.

"That stallion of yours - Midnight you single - handedly raised him I hear? " Rum asked Shelley.

"Yes. I even bottle-fed that young colt…and it's funny…he never bucked with me on his back."

"I know. They tell me not too many people can even approach him unless you're with them… just like a guard-dog, " one of the men added.

"And on the Fourth of July, you always win the big race with that horse against the three town's best riders, "another listener stated.

"Yes, said Shelley, "'Night' is the finest of all the horses on the range."

"Not only is Night a beautiful, black horse, but he was born at midnight," Shelley told the Rum family as she sat and ate a late breakfast with them.

"Yeah," said Naaman, "as I recall, that Pal-amino that Carson rides was born a few days later. The kid kept calling him a pony, but the younger kids couldn't say 'pony', they said 'Coney' and that has been his name ever since. Since Carson was recuperating at the time he bargained for Coney, and he became his horse."

As they had stated earlier, no man knew Midnight like Shelley, but they failed to realize that as Kirby Carson was healing, he would limp from the farmhouse to the house ranch and talk softly to Midnight like a horse-whisperer and give him treats like carrots and apples and sometimes sugar. Carson kept this friendship with Midnight a secret between he and the horse. He figured that if at any time Shelley might not be available, someone should be able to handle the stallion. Midnight got quite used to Carson because of their secret meetings.

The ranchers figured that if Carson was to pick a horse from the horse-Ranch it would probably be 'fog', a fine gray mustang, but Carson's choice was the Palomino, since he couldn't have Midnight.

As Shelley was about to leave the farmhouse, she saw a cloud of dust on the trail leading to the farmhouse.

"Carson is coming! "She declared to the Rum family. As Carson arrive and dismounted, he greeted Shelley again and said to Mrs. Rum,

"I'm ready for that home cookin' now."

"Her baked bread is still the best in the county," Naaman said.

"Come right in and participate."

Back in town, the people were still upset because of the bank robbery. They began to point the finger at anyone they might deem suspicious.

"Those bank robbers could be far out of town by now and don't have to be anyone around here," one person stated. "Yeah, but who else would know about the payroll?" another one added.

"Let the deputy handle it," said another. "That's what he's being paid for."

Still another bystander griped, "Can we even trust him? Some of us still feel like he was the one who released some of those jailbirds."

Why anyone would suspect their deputy?

There was a stagecoach hold up two months before and the townspeople grab the first man they suspected and some of them tried to hang him without a trial. The deputy, still the only law in Gun-Fire Valley, was on the other end of town when he heard what was going on.

"Carson is coming!" Someone yelled to the ringleader of the mob.

"Hold on there!" yelled Carson. "They'll be no illegal hangin' around here!" As he's speedily dismounted, Carson grabbed the young man from the mob—leaders and hustled him into the jail.

"That's OK," one of mob leaders said "Judge 'Hang 'em' Haney is making his rounds this way. He'll do the hangin'!"

Carson found out later from the passenger on the stagecoach that the holdup man had lost a part of his spur. The young man the mob was about to hang had both his spurs intact. The mob still convinced that they had the right man drummed up some trumped-up charges on him to save face! Judge Thomas Thornton Haney, known as 'Hang 'em Haney'– not because he was known to be a hanging judge, but because he had heard much of the antics of King Thompus and was determined that if he ever got hard evidence against Thompus, he would hang him and his hat from the gallows. True to form, he arrived at his appointed time checking on the scattered sites of unsettled, half settled territories of his district and various counties under his jurisdiction.

The young prisoner was quite nervous as the judge stepped into the sheriff's office. Reading Carson, and Judge Haney hung his robe behind the rifle rack and asked the deputy if he could leave it there with his luggage piece, for he was seeking a room in the hotel. The judge wanted to go over some procedures with the town's only lawman.

When the judge left the jail to grab a steak at the town's eatery, he left his robe and luggage with Carson. The black robe gave Carson an idea. Knowing that the young suspect didn't stand much of a chance for a fair trial, Carson draped the judge's robe over his face and rounded himself as much as he could, concealing his face. He then unlocked the jail cell and muffling his voice, he instructed the young man to spread the word as he went, that a mysterious man in black, with a black mask, and riding a black horse came in suddenly, overpowering the deputy, and releasing him. The young man started out quickly in search of a horse for his getaway. When the judge returned to the jail, Carson was getting up off the floor, holding his head as if he was just coming to from being knocked unconscious. The judge had no problem believing Carson story, but the townspeople had their doubts.

Ever since that event, most of the people wanted to think that their lawman was innocent of such a deed, even though they, too, wanted a fair trial for the young man. Someone wanted to applaud his escape but dared not show their feelings on the matter. The mob leaders and their followers were totally against Carson, but they had no evidence. To take some of the tension away, Carson later downed a black outfit and borrowed Midnight and went to the other two towns releasing men from jail cells and riding off as the 'Mystery Rider'.

He would spread his reputation by holding up a few stagecoaches. In order to do that, the guard must be disposed of, so Carson would spread large tree branches in the road so the guard would have to get down and move them. While he was doing this, the mystery rider would surprise him, hold him at gun point, and command the stagecoach driver to throw down the strongbox.

Who would then suspect a deputy of the law of such antics? None of the horses were fast enough to catch Midnight, and no one would even consider Shelley Weston –the only one, they thought, was able to ride that stallion. They all said it was a tall man on a black horse. Shelley could not possibly fit the bill.

While Gun-Fire Valley buzzed busily because of the bank robbery, GunBelt had its own problems. The gunman from Oklahoma, Wyoming, Missouri, and other areas that Johnny 'Sweetshot' Logan had contacted to settle in Delton were moving in also on the town of GunBelt. Their presence also kept the townspeople on edge even though the weekend fights that often lead to shootings were on a decline. With that many gunmen, the regular cowboys held their peace most of the time.

One day a former gunman and outlaw returned to the western town of GunBelt and was greeted by the town's bully. Big Pete Briggs knew nothing of the newcomer, but being the troublemaker that he was, he harassed a stranger into a fight. Now Pete was the town's leading boxer and wrestler when the three towns gathered for the Fourth of July activities. The stranger was Paul Billard. His brothers had been shot down by Sheriff Band's posse. Paul had escaped and moved eastward to avoid the law. Now he returned to find a challenge with the town's bully. Billard was not looking for trouble. His return west was to see if his stolen monies were yet hidden away where he and his brothers had hidden it.

As he is forced into a fist fight, he knew it would have been so much easier to draw his six guns and shoot the boaster.

However, since Billard was pretty good with his fist, he decided to take a chance since he wanted to take the more peaceable route. It turned out to be a big mistake on part of Billard. The big man hit him in the jaw, picked him up, and threw him across a saloon table. When Billard recovered, he found himself flying by the hitching post against a horse drinking trough.

Gathering his thoughts as he pulled himself up from the ground, Billard walking away, with his pride a little hurt, figuring that Briggs had plenty of gun happy friends to back any other play he might make.

Settling down in his hotel, Paul Billard began his vengeful plan. *"This,"* he thought, *"would not go unanswered."* He had a close connection with the dreaded Rinald Delton, and he was certainly going to send for him.

Billard first part of his plan was get to know the town people and their officials. Since there was no real law in the town, his plan was to get himself appointed Sheriff. With Rinald Delton's help, they will clean up the town of GunBelt. The residents of GunBelt were desperate for some kind of change.

Since Sheriff Sidney Bands, from Nevada, was yet forming posse after posse on his quest to change the image of the lawless towns, Paul Billard was to do his part in Delton. Sending funds to his family in Indiana under his other alias 'Rex Harding', Paul Bolton alias Paul Billard awaited his moment to move on reforming the town.

The July 4th festivities took place in the wide-open area called the 'Festivities Grounds' where the three towns gathered to celebrate. The people noted that not only did the Colonel's horse 'Midnight', ridden by Shelley Weston, continue to win the horse races, Shelley herself was a pretty good sharpshooter on the gun range. Some of the gunmen displayed their skills with the six-gun, however the faster draw was not always the most accurate. As a matter of fact, seldom was the man with the fastest draw the most accurate. Never-the-less, the regular arms bearers dared not challenge the most disliked gunmen.

Carson, riding Coney, gave Midnight a good run but the black stallion always showed why he was the champion. His gun play was quite respectable, but since the gunmen weren't causing any trouble, Carson found no cause to challenge any of them. The cattlemen and the sheepmen even joined the fun and gave little trouble. Yes, they were some fights and scuffles that broke out, but very little arrests were made because of it.

The song and dance portion of the festivities were the most peaceful and square dancing was center stage. The fireworks, target shooting, and livestock calling were the noisiest.

The boxing and wrestling matches held excitement with Big Pete Briggs against Curt Sherley. Carson even participated in these two competitions. Showing that he was quite the man to contend with, because of this he was becoming a well-respected lawman.

Curt Sherley, a boxer and a wrestler, was the brother to Matt and Gus Sherley, outlaws who warred against Thompus' nephews the Porter brothers. There was always trouble when these factors came together.

The townspeople wanted Kirby Carson to send for Ben Masters to help clear up some of the strife they had to live with. The towns were lawless and unestablished legally, but the mayors, officials, and deputy kept some kind of control. The bad guys always realized that they were in an outlaw haven, so they had to keep a low profile to keep the big guns of the law from bearing down upon these territories. Of course, when cooler heads do not prevail, trouble runs rapidly.

So, all –in– all, the July 4th celebrations seemed to be the most celebrated for the people of Thompus Towns. Even the Indians would perform with dances, tomahawk throws, bow and arrows, horseback tricks, ceremonial dances, tumbling, and other displays. It was the wild weekend that brewed the most trouble bringing drinking, brawling and problems.

Paul Billard was keeping a low profile because the determined Sheriff Bands was on the prowl in GunBelt. A plan was being hatched by Billard once he heard of how the mystery rider was letting men free from jail and he was seeking revenge on the Sheriff for his posse had gunned down his brothers. So, he figured if he could dress up in black each time the sheriff arrested someone, he could at least harass him until he could come up with a plan to kill him. Sheriff Bands was wounded in his shoot out with the Boltons, but he survived and became determined to set his life's work on capturing outlaws. Billard now planned to release everyone Bands could catch. The original mystery rider would doubtlessly be blamed if Billard's plan worked. The Porter Brothers —nephew of King Thompus had also wanted to rule the town.

The Porter Brothers of Gunbelt, four nephews of King Thompus, were running the outlaw towns with Thompus himself pulling the strings from prison. The four gunmen kept the towns folks on edge. They tried to emulate the four Bolton brothers who were dreaded outlaw's years before. Gerry Winson, who was raised with the Porters, was their foster-sister.

She was just handy with six-guns as the boys were and she found out as a teenager that she had a brother by the name of Bart Winson. When Bart learned where he could find his sister, he came to Gunbelt to unite with her.

The Porter boys didn't care much for Bart. He was a loser and somewhat of a troublemaker. That's all the town needed—another troublemaker.

In Gun-Fire Valley, the townspeople had gotten Ben Masters and Judge Haney to return and to help the deputy to solve the bank robbery. Carson was the only local law for the three towns and the people felt unsecured. Judge Haney directed the people to elect a mayor officially and select a sheriff. Kirby Carson considered running for sheriff since he was doing the job anyway, but Judge Haney brought along two men that were to be considered as well.

When the first choice to be sheriff, learned of all the ruthless outlaws in the three towns, he became quite skeptical and could not make up his mind as to whether he really wanted the job or not.

The other man was Sidney Bands. He was already a sheriff who was more of a roving lawman and who would go wherever the money was the biggest draw. Bands was known for his trick-holster, but in reality, he was never able to perfect the spring-action, but the outlaws and the people never knew that. No one wanted to challenge its authenticity. As a result, Lee Venon Rose became mayor of Delton, and Kirby Carson eventually became sheriff of Gun-Fire Valley.

In GunBelt, Paul Billard became sheriff with Rinald Delton as his deputy. The Porter brothers, to keep their Uncle Thompus up on everything, had to establish themselves in Delton as well as GunBelt. This wasn't easy because the three Sherley brothers were there and always troublesome.

Now mayor of Delton, L. Venon Rose (as he liked to be called) was a flamboyant playboy. He and John 'Sweetshot' Logan competed for the ladies' attention. Rose, a few years older than Logan, kept a well-trimmed, partial beard and mustache. Logan was clean-shaven with a slender mustache. Logan was both well dressed and always sporting a well-designed vest.

The mayor used his position to catch Logan in any illegal act that he could get him put away. It verily came to pass that Logan went too far and Judge Haney was making his rounds at the right time. Mayor L. Venon Rose made his move, and he was sent to prison for three years. With Logan gone, another man took over the saloon and Rose's competitor was Kirby Carson, a womanizer in his own right. Carson's eye was mainly on

Shelley Weston. Rose had an eye for Dolly 'Doll-face', the town doctor's nurse. Dolly couldn't decide on Rose or Logan, but she enjoyed flirting with Carson.

With law and order being set up in each town, all the townspeople had to be concerned about was the Indians on each side of Gun-Fire Valley. Chief Montus 'Big Mountain' ruled one side of the mountain range and a younger Chief 'Flaming Eagle' ruled by the other side. With connection Indian connection, there was some peace, but Flaming Eagle was not so easy to co-operate when it came to various regulations set up by the towns' officials.

On the last July 4th celebration, Chief Flaming Eagle came riding as if out of nowhere on a horse named Night-Wild and almost over-took Shelley Weston riding Midnight. Flaming Eagle rode pass Roy Slim riding his horse "Dust" and by-passed Kirby, Carson riding Coney. The scoring officials claimed that the Indian chief did not start at the proper starting gate and refused to honor him with the second-place prize. This caused bad blood between the chief, some of his people, and the townspeople. Every now and then a band of young warriors would pull a raid on some of the settlers and rattle the whole town. The stage-couch line was interrupted by Indians. The passengers were robbed and harassed, but none were killed. The Calvary had to be called in when things got too hectic. With treaties broken and renegades on the loose the only thing that finally calmed the air was threats to move the tribes to reservations.

Chief Montus made visits to the prison to talk to King Thompus. Eventually Chief Flaming Eagle was persuaded to go with Chief Montus for a pow-wow. Peace with the Indians finally occurred.

One day a band of Indians were watching the stagecoach from a hillside. Suddenly a rider on a black horse with a black cape and dressed in black with a mask over his face came riding up and stopped the stagecoach. The stagecoach driver and his guard were taken completely by surprise. They had seen the Indians and were concentrating on them when the Mystery Rider appeared. One of the passengers pulled his gun from his briefcase and fired at the rider, striking him in the shoulder. Almost falling from his horse, the masked rider rode away.

When the stagecoach arrived at Gun-Fire Valley the Indians followed. They wanted to hear the passengers' account of the incident. As soon as the townspeople heard what had happened with the stagecoach, they knew to look for a wounded man. Those that had suspected Kirby Carson to be the Mystery Rider could hardly wait to see if he was wounded. At the time, Carson could not be found. The crowd was divided in their opinions and was beginning to get unruly. Suddenly the cry "Carson is coming." Was heard and the crowd stood back as their sheriff rode up.

"What's the trouble here?" Asked Carson as he dismounted.

At first the people were silent and then they all began to speak at once. Seeing Carson was not shot, a sigh of relief was heard. The passengers followed Carson to his office at the jail and gave their account of what had transpired. The Indians listened entirely and then mounted up and rode off.

Carson and the lawmen now had another crime to solve. A group of former posse members from Nevada had fallen in love with their work running down outlaws. Carson had made it clear to the gunmen of the three towns that even though they may be wanted men, as long as they kept their noses clean, they would have no problem from him. The Nevada group was made up of vigilant- minded men needing a badge-carrying man to lead them. Sidney Bands was unusually called upon for the task. Carson sometimes led the group. Whenever the hunted were found, the Nevada group would turn joyfully to peaceful surroundings until the call went out for a readymade posse. Ordinarily a lawman needing a posse would have formed one of volunteering townsmen. This group would have men stationed in various areas with watchful eyes and listening ear for the call of a needed posse.

Even if a posse was already formed, the Nevada group would join them for the thrill of the chase. At this time no posse was being formed, but the spies were ever alert.

Sheriff Carson was making a call on the town doctor. The nurse answered the door.

"Hi, man with the tin-star," Dolly 'Doll-face' said, as she opened the door.

"Hello, Doll-face," answered Carson as he entered the doctor's office.

"I'm looking for your most recent patients. Where's Doc?"

"He's out, Tin-Star. May I help you in any way?" She said with a flirting smile.

"Yeah," said Carson, gently pushing her aside.

"Your recent patient. Who were they?"

"Well, there was a man with a bad limp and then one with a rope-burn on his neck. I think he had escaped from Judge Haney...and uh, I think he was Gerry Winson's brother."

"What was he here for?" Carson asked.

"Isn't that doctor and patient business, or something like that?" Dolly griped.

"I'm the law, Doll-face. Now, what was he here for?" he asked.

Dolly hesitated. Then she smiled slowly.

"Where is the Doc, Dolly? Where is he?" asked Carson.

"He'll be back soon. Won't you have a seat?"

"No! I'll be back. You could get in trouble withholding information from the law." Carson said.

"All right! Okay. You would've found out anyways." She said, "He had a slug in his left shoulder."

Carson left without another word. Dolly called out after him, "Do you still want to see the doc?" Carson saluted her and rode away.

Finding Bart Winson wasn't hard. Carson got his new deputy, Roy Slim, and went to the town's boarding house. There in the lobby was Winson, arm in a sling and a battle of rum in his hand.

"You Bart Winson?" Carson asked.

"You know I am, Sheriff. I introduced myself as soon as I hit town. Isn't that proper in your vicinity?"

"I need to know why your arm is in a sling?" Carson said.

"Is there a law around here against a man with his arm in a sling? Bart griped.

"It depends on why it's in a sling, I reckon," Carson stated.

"I lifted something the wrong way and strained it," Bart said.

"Sheriff," said Bart. "I'm not the only man in town with his arm in a sling. You gonna question each one you see?"

"What color is your horse, Mr. Winson?" asked Carson.

"I ride a bay mare. I don't own a horse yet. I borrowed my sister's bay 'til I can buy my own. I'm eyeballing that fine mustang they call 'Cloud', but the Colonel is asking too much for him. Cloud is a fine ride. You thru with me Sheriff? I am about to kill this rum-bottle and get me some sleep."

"I'll be back, Mr. Wilson," said Carson. "I'll be back."

A few days later, Carson and Roy Slim noticed several men with their arms carried gently in a sling. Questioning them one by one, their answers made little sense. One young man finally said, "A guy offered me a silver dollar if I could wear this thing for three days."

"There are several black horses in these three towns. It could've been either one of 'em." Roy Slim said to Carson.

"I know!" griped Roy.

"The silver dollars! How many is being handed out? What was in the stage hold-up?"

"There's one thing wrong with that idea, Roy," answered Carson. "The masked rider didn't get the money."

"Uh, yeah… that's right." Roy said thinking deeply.

"Yeah! But if Winson is our man, he could've borrowed anyone's black horse, or with a silver dollar, rented a horse... I really think he's the man. He's the only one treated with a shoulder wound. I'm sure of it, Roy. I just need proof. I need him to slip up. Hmmm. Dolly 'Doll-face' Dolly sure seemed to be holding back on telling on him. I think I'll pay her a personal visit." Carson said to his deputy.

"She has quite an eye for the guys."

"Yeah," said Roy, "Even you."

"I'm not countin' on that," said Carson.

When Carson showed up at Dolly's apartment, Bart was just leaving. "Howdy Sheriff," he said hesitantly. Carson touched the rim of his hat and walked in.

"Come in, Tin-star," Dolly said "...Oh! You're already in, aren't you?" Carson pulled up a chair and sat down.

"Come in! Have a seat! Make yourself comfortable," she snarled. "What do you want, Sheriff?"

"Oh," said Carson, "I thought I was 'Tin-Star'!"

"State your business, I have to go to work. The doc is not a patient man," Dolly said.

"Well, I told you I'd be back," Carson said, raising from his feet.

"That was Bart Winson. What's he doing here? This isn't the doc's office."

"None of your.... oh, that's right. You are the law. I guess everything is your business," Dolly said. "I understand you are taking time with Shelley Weston. Does that cover some of your duties, Tin-Star?"

"Well, I happen to know that a certain schoolteacher is waiting her turn for a fling with you."

"Listen Dolly, I..." As Carson took her by the shoulders, he noted three silver dollars on her dresser. "Where'd you get the shiny ones?" He asked.

"Look, Kirby, I have to go now. Come back tonight when I'm off work.

"Oh, now it's Kirby... Okay. I will be back, Doll-face," he stated as he departed.

Waiting outside and unobserved, Carson watched Dolly leave her apartment, walk across the street to the doctor's office, and put a black horse tied at the hitching post in front of the doctor's office.

As Carson rode out to the Rum farm hoping to find Shelley Weston there, he was greeted by the four Indian Braves that were witnesses to the attempted stage-coach hold-up.

"It's Man Kirs," the Braves leader said to the others. Carson was well-known to the tribes as the lawman they called 'Man Kirs'.

"How!" said they in their former salute to each other, "we watch the trails and open range. We do our part to keep peace in our area.

"Yes," answered Carson. "This is good."

"We see many strange things. Mask man we call Karrah-Vanno. He tried to hold up stage. Karrah-Vanno catch shot from stage window. Ride away swiftly. We follow."

"Yeah, I'm looking for him."

"We keep watch. Things keep things peaceful. Chief say if we do this, soldiers stay away. Not drive us off our land to one day call 'reservation'! We no like."

"I informed your chief that we would do all we could to keep the soldiers away, but it's only so much we can do. We'll keep trying. So far, it's working. Chief Montus seems to be doing his part to hold things down, but Chief Flaming Eagle gets a little restless. He could thwart our efforts," Carson said to the Braves.

"Chief Big Mountain… He try to keep reason with Flaming Eagle – sometimes Flaming Eagle listen – sometimes Flaming Eagle ride off. Many braves agree with Flaming Eagle – still we want no trouble," the Indian said. Carson saluted the Braves in route toward the Rum farm.

As Naaman Rum and his son sat at the dinner table, one of the young men looked out the window and seeing a cloud of dust, he exclaimed, "Carson is coming!"

"Yeah," said Naaman, "I told him he was always welcome to our dinner table."

While continuing their meal after greeting Carson and setting his meal before him, outlaws became the topic of discussion. "The law is increasing in our various areas by guys like the Porter brothers seemed to be trying to slow the process," Carson stated.

"Yeah," one of the Rums sons added, "They want to be like the Bolton brothers. They had a tragic end. It's not worth it."

"The feud with those Sherley brothers seemed to be heating up," another son added, "It's rather scary."

"With Thompus locked up and now Sweet-Shot Logan, the situation isn't getting any better. There are just too many lawless men in these parts," Carson stated.

"How did they actually catch up with Thompus?" Naaman asked Carson.

"Some of his own men turned on him. They were supposed to take the fall, but they wiggled out of it. The Porters are his kinfolks and one of the Sherley brothers was with the man that ratted Thompus out," said Carson. "You can see why the feud stays hot."

"A lot of people like Thompus. They said he never miss church or Bible study. I don't get it," Rum's third son stated.

"He's got a lot of smarts, that guy. Dancehalls, saloons, telegram – telegraph office, hotels, and above all, churches, and schools," Naaman said. "Soon this area will get notoriety… If the outlaws don't spoil it for us."

"General stores, strong jail, yeah," say Carson "we have it all. Railroads, soon a slaughter-house – we can stop sending beef east for processing. When I turn lawing a loose, I think I'll settle for farm life like you. Life is grand living on a farm."

"Yeah," laughed Naaman. "Yeah! Grand."

O n Carson's return to the jail, he found that his deputy Roy Slim had arrested Curt Sherley.

"It was almost a fight," Roy told Carson. "I got there in time to break it up."

"Any trouble locking him up?" Carson asked.

"Naw. He came along peacefully. I'll hold him long enough for him to cool off.

"Okay," said Carson "I'm going to go see Doll-face."

"Right," said Roy "Bring back some convincing evidence."

As Carson headed down the street, he hadn't gone far before Roy Slim came running and calling to him.

"Hey Kirby. Wait up," he yelled "great time o' day!"

"What is it, Roy?" ask Carson.

"That Curt Sherley had a habit of talking to himself. I heard him laughing in mumbling something. I think he mentioned the bank."

"Yeah?" asked Carson "Look! Find out what he likes to drink and get him a bottle from the saloon."

"Right!" Said Roy "He should really talk once he's good and drunk.

"Well, don't let him get too drunk or he might fall asleep before he says anything pertinent...unless he also talks in his sleep," stated Carson.

"Right," said Roy "Right! I'm right on it."

As Carson continued down the street, Dolly was leaving the doctor's office for the day. Catching up with her, he said "May I walk with you, lovely lady? I may have an interesting tale to tell you."

"Come right on, Tin-star. I'm always interested in hearing something new." Dolly James answered.

As they enter Dolly's building, Carson noticed Bart Winson standing by the saloon door and watching him "You have admirers everywhere," he said to Dolly.

"Oh," she said. "You noticed Bart, did you?"

"I did," said Carson. "I think the whole town notices him. Anytime he's in town, I hear about it."

"He lives in Gunbelt, but a few miles is nothing for him to travel. He sometimes rides a different horse each trip." Said Dolly.

"Even a black one, I'm told," said Carson. "I want you to be careful of him."

"I'm going to give you a silver dollar not to worry about me and him," Dolly said.

"Yeah," said Carson. "I notice you have a couple of them lying around."

"Sure," said Dolly. "The doc has a habit of paying me in silver dollars. You might find a few lying around anywhere in my apartment."

"Winson isn't a working man. He carries silver dollars. He could be robbing you every time he visits—or is he robbing the doctor?!"

"No," said Dolly. "I've been keeping him supplied in silver bucks ever since we met. I guess I got a crush on him."

"Like I have on you, huh?" Asked Carson as he turned her and kissed her.

As Dolly gently pulled away from the embrace, she said, "You'd be a real catch. Tin-Star, but my heart is wild. I have to consider my options."

"Take your time, beautiful. You certainly want to make the right choice," Carson said, "But Bart Winson? Why in the world Bart Winson? He's been nothing but trouble since he's been around."

"He brings an air of excitement into my life," Dolly said.

Mayor Lee Venon Rose decided to call a meeting of the three sheriffs of the towns because he had heard that the Nevada group was on their way to Belton. "That group of vigilantes got together to shoot you men down for support," Rose told the Sheriffs.

"Now, wait," said Sidney Bands. "I was a Nevada sheriff when my brother was shot down by outlaws. Those men were mostly friends our family were close too. They wanted to see those outlaws caught as bad as I did, so they have been following me ever since."

"A sheriff's jurisdiction is only in the town he was elected to," said Paul Billard to Bands. "How are you authorized to go beyond like you do?"

"I know," said Bands, "well I am now, as the roving sheriff. When the governor heard my story and realized my plight, he authorized me to go above and beyond the call of duty to pull any punches or whatever it took to bring these guys to justice.

"You may as well be a US Marshall," Carson said. "They're the only ones that can do that."

"Well actually, I am one unofficially. I guess I got hooked on the sheriff title. It just seems to pack a harder punch."

"Never-the-less", said Rose, "those men have a reputation of gunning a man down without much of a chance to surrender."

"That's a stretch, Mr. Mayor," said Bands, "I'll defend those guys with my life last bullet."

"So why are they coming here," asked Carson. "We seemed to be shaping things up without a party of their nature."

"I'm sure they have their reasons, answered Bands.

"I'll question them when they get here," Bands continued "I'll get to the bottom of this."

Days went by and the Nevada group never showed. Mayor Rose and Kirby Carson figure Bands sent them word not to come. When the stagecoach arrived, two brothers arrived in Delton. Two blonde haired young men who were making their name in a new place. Like Bart Winson, one of the twins was a troublemaker. The other was mild mannered and reasonable. Shelley Weston greeted the twins and escorted them to the boarding house where they would live until they settled elsewhere.

Shelley was spending more and more time with the mild-mannered twin as days went by. The other twin was getting more and more involved with the criminal element of Delton.

"As different as night and day" he kept hearing from the townspeople when they observe the twins. "The Dawson twins bared watching," the townspeople would say to Sheriff Bands and to the mayor. "The one brother is all right, but the other one my, my."

When Kirby Carson went to talk to Doll-face Dolly, she said to him "Instead of keeping such an eye on Bart, you would do well to watch the new cowboy."

"Bands is watching him Doll-face," Carson said

"Oh, I don't mean the rowdy one I mean the one that is sweeping your girlfriend off her feet. I'm sure you are the last one to know. Are you being moved out?"

"Hmmm!" thought Carson. "I haven't been to Delton in a few days. Maybe I've stayed away too long.'"

"You could, Tin-star," said Dolly ""I've seen the guy. You could lose."

When Kirby Carson entered the jail office, he found a prisoner still jailed. "I thought you only wanted to hold him long enough to get him sobered up," he said to his pal and deputy Roy Slim.

"The more I keep him drinking, said Roy "the more he runs his mouth. He even talks in his sleep. He and his brothers robbed the bank all right. All we have to do is find where they stashed the cash."

"That's great, Roy" said Carson, "we'll have to put a tail on the other two, and I know just who to put on their trail. Chief Big Mountain has a couple of scouts I can use. I'll be back."

During Carson's ride to the mountain range that overlooked Gun-Fire Valley, he passed the area known as 'the edge'. The edge was somewhat of a dumping ground for when the Indians would slaughter a buffalo, their remains would be dumped there. This procedure would draw wolves, bears, mountain lions, and any other meat-eating creature including vultures. The edge was on the outskirts of the Indian camps and far enough away not to disturb the towns or the Indians.

As Carson rolled by, a pack of wolves was tearing away at a carcass of an old horse. "*The Indians must have hauled it there rather than buried it*", thought Carson. When he reached the Indian stronghold, he mentioned the old horse to Chief Montus.

"My people would not do such a thing. A horse is a noble animal. We would burn him as we were at a noble break," said Montus said to Carson.

"I need a favor from you, Chief," Carson uttered.

"Speak Man-Kir. You are my friend," said the chief.

"I need the eyes of the best scout. There are men that robbed from our people. I think I know who these men are. I need a tracker to follow them,"

"I will send Little Horse and Two Feather. They will follow your men." granting his request.

Matt and Gus Sherley were getting impatient and decided their brother Curt had been held long enough. When Carson and the two Braves arrived at the jail, the three brothers were leaving. The timing was just right. All the sheriffs had to do was show the Braves the three men they were to secretly follow.

As the days went on, Carson was training for a boxing match with Curt Sherley. The winner was to fight Big Pete Briggs, the town's champion on the Fourth of July.

When the boxing date arrived, the crowd gathered at the open area where the ring was set up. The Sherley brothers went to get more money to bet on their brother. The Braves followed. As the bout began, Dolly yelled from the front row "Go get them Tin-star. I might be your price."

By the second round, the Sherley brothers returned and raised the betting stakes. The Braves sat back and watched the fight. The first round was pretty even. The second round, Curt was winning. The third row, the sheriff was staging a strong come back. Suddenly, as the fourth round began, Ted Dawson arrived with Shelley Weston on his arm. This caught Carson's attention more than the Sherley brothers and before he knew it, he was catching a hard right to the body. His arm draped over Curt's shoulders leaving him open to three more body shots.

Slumping backward reaching for the ropes, Carson found himself falling thru the ropes and landing out of the ring at the feet of Dolly Doll-face and Mayor Lee Venon Rose. "You're not gonna win Dolly as a prize, Sheriff," Rose said.

"You might not win at all." Dolly (Doll-face) James smiled softly.

Carson staggered to his feet and looking excitedly around, made his way back to the apron of the ring. He managed to crawl back into the ring before the count of fifteen. So, hanging on his opponent, he managed to survive the fourth round. The two Indian scouts hurried to Carson's corner to tell him of their findings.

"Keep an eye on those brothers," Carson said to Roy Slim. "I'll take care of this one."

The bell rang for round five and Carson's eyes fell on Shelley Weston sitting in the crowd with Ted Dawson.

"Wow!" exclaimed Roy as he watched Curt Sherley connect on the sheriff. "If you're gonna take care of him, you've got a funny way of doing it."

Carson staggered back and gathered his bearings. Blocking the next few punches from Sherley. Carson began to connect lefts and rights and finally Curl Sherley dropped to the canvas. The count went to ten and the sheriff was declared the winner.

"You had me worried there for a while, man!" Roy said to Carson.

"Yeah," said Carson. "Yeah. Come on. Let's see what Two Feather and Little Horse found out."

A few hours later after rewarding the Indians scouts, Carson and Roy began putting their plan together to trap the bank robbers.

"Some of the people won't be surprised when we present the evidence on these buzzards. They suspected them anyway," Roy told Carson.

"Yeah," said Carson. "I know. Look, I've got something I gotta take care of. I'll see you later."

As night was approaching, Carson rode out to the Colonel's horse range. He could see the Rum family house 80 yards away. Carson went into the barn and talked with Midnight. "Ready for the night ride, old buddy?" Carson saddled Midnight and took his black outfit from a secret hiding place. "Tonight, the Mystery Rider rides…" And he rode away into the night.

In Carson's mind, he meant to spy on Shelley Weston, but as he rode, he was thinking, *"Maybe I should capture those brothers as the mask rider and give the Mystery Rider a good name and one to be feared by the outlaws. Well, first Shelley—my love then, maybe and perhaps, the Sherley brothers."*

As it turned out, spying on Shelley Weston was easier than catching the bank robbers. The Sherley brothers were already making plans to leave the state. If Carson was to catch them, he would have to move fast.

The Mystery Rider found Shelley Weston talking with Sheriff Bands and Ted Dawson. Bands was nervous and had a mind to move on.

Sitting in one area was just not to his liking. There was a pretty qualified man ready to step in and take his place as sheriff, but he couldn't make up his mind if he really wanted the job.

He was the same man they had talked to before.

As Kirby Carson spies on his lady love, the Indian scout spot the Karrah-Vanno. "Let us go to Man-Kir and tell him of this," Little Horse said to Two Feather. Not realizing that Karrah-Vanno is Carson, the scouts headed for the jail to report their findings.

On the way back to mount Midnight, Carson was thinking to himself *"I guess I should have made some kind of commitment. I may have lost this girl."* As Carson climbed into the saddle, he heard riders.

"It's him. The Masked Mystery Rider!" They shouted. "Get him! Get him!"

Carson rode swiftly around two buildings and dismounted. Running into an apartment building, he was about to unmask himself when he ran into three Dancehall girls. The girls began to scream. The pursuing men outside heard the commotion and ran in. Surrounded by the man, Carson began to fight his way out, but was quickly grabbed by the other men who were coming in the other door.

"Okay," one of them said "we got him. Now let's see who is behind the mask."

Carson bucked and kicked, so the men were not able to get to his mask. "Okay, I know," said one of the men "get one of these girls to unmask him he won't kick one of them."

As one of the Dancehall girls drew near to remove Carson's mask, he refused to kick her. "It's the sheriff! by golly, it's sheriff Carson. Now, how do you explain this?"

"Now wait" said Carson "let's not draw any rush conclusions!"

"Here comes the deputy," one man said. "Lock up the sheriff. He can explain himself behind bars." So, Roy Slim led his buddy off to the jail.

As the man walked up the street to the jail, suddenly a masked rider on the back of a horse rode by shooting at the air.

"What?" Ask the man. "What in the world is going on around here? Who is that? Who is really the mask rider?"

"That's what I was trying to tell you," Carson said to the man. "I was setting a trap for the real bandit. You guys spoiled it."

"The sheriff is right," said Roy. "We have a plan that we are working on. Mount up, man! Let's catch that Mystery Rider. Carson was right. He did show up tonight."

As Roy Slim rode off into the night as puzzled as the rest of the man, Carson stood in the doorway watching them ride.

About an hour later, Shelley Weston rode up to the jail on Coney. As she entered the sheriff's office, she charged up to Carson saying, "You got a lot of explaining to do Mister!"

"And so have you," smiled Carson.

"How in the world did Midnight let you ride him. Why are you dressed like that! What are you… wait a minute…Carson… are you? Oh, my! What have I done?"

"Hold on, young lady. One question at a time. I was in a real pickle. When you rode by shooting and leading those men on a wild goose chase, well, thanks! I knew it was you as soon as I saw Midnight. You work fast. I knew they wouldn't catch you."

"When I came outside to see what the racket was about, Midnight came up to me. When I saw them leading you away, well, I felt I owed you something, so I grabbed the first dark thing I could find and draped it around me and well, you know. When I got to the barn, there stood Coney. I knew then for sure it was you that you…you are the original… I mean… Midnight no one can catch him. Oh, Kirby I… I… Please, tell me."

As Carson began to tell Shelley of his exploits, Roy Slim and the other men arrived. "We lost him, sheriff. He was too fast for us."

As a man with their ways and Roy Slim settled down in the sheriff's office, Kirby and Shelley stepped outside. As they continued the conversation, Kirby got around to asking, "this new fellow Ted Dawson, I've been hearing about. Just how does he rate with you?

"Oh," said Shelley "well he's…he's…he's a wonderful guy. Well you seemed to be hitting it off together. You know, Kirby, I care a lot for you… But, well, you know, neither of us has made any type of commitment and well, I've actually falling for the guy… and… he loves me… I… I'm sorry."

"Ha! Well," say Kirby, "I am… I'm not sure what to say. I thought… I mean, I know we had something you and I…"

"Yes," said Shelley, "we certainly did…And … And maybe we still do. When I saw them dragging you off to jail, I just knew I had to do something. I don't know, Kirby. Ted is… Well, Ted is… He is…"

"It's alright," Kirby spoke. "Maybe time will tell how real… Or what…" He embraced her gently, and then he walked away leaving her to ponder.

Shortly after, Ted Dawson came around the corner. "Where did you go?" He asked her. "I looked around and I was alone. I'm not used to being alone since you've come into my life." Shelley didn't answer and the two of them walked away.

The next day, Roy Slim asked Kirby, "What is the plan? I'm still baffled over last night. The men believe what I told them but some of them are still skeptical."

"I'm not surprised," said Kirby. "I guess I would be too. I know you didn't know what to think seeing me dressed up like the mystery rider. I had to do some fast thinking and when that rider showed up, well, I was given a reprieve."

"You're my pal, Roy. I've told Shelley and I guess I can tell you. The original Mystery Rider was me…. and I'll tell you why I did it."

So, after disclosing his secret to Roy, Roy had but one question. "You eventually robbed the stage? I don't understand."

"That was to throw people off. No one would believe that an honest deputy would lose prisoners and hold up stagecoaches, so even though some still suspected me, their suspicions dwindled." Carson said.

The town was buzzing about the two Mystery Riders. Bart Winson thought to himself, "if I had shown up, there would have been three."

When the four Indian Braves that had witnessed the stagecoach hold-up attempt, they said among themselves that they knew who the particular rider was, and it was not "Man-Kirs" as they called Carson.

"This man we followed he was shot. When he removed his mask, his face was still covered. This refers to the heavy bearded Bart Winson wore so proudly. When the Indians told this to Kirby Carson, he thanked them and let them know he was planning to spring a trap to catch Winson.

After the Braves rode away, Roy Slim asked the sheriff one more question concerning his own stagecoach hold up.

"What about the money? You surely didn't spend it."

"No," said Carson. "I have it stashed away at the boarding house. When we catch Winson, we'll turn it in. That way, it'll look like he was the original Mystery Rider."

"That could get him hanged. Are you sure that is what we want?"

"Hmmmmm," Carson thought. "Well, I'm still working on that part of the plan. I don't reckon he deserves hangin."

As Kirby Carson told his latest venture to his friend and deputy Roy Slim, Roy remarked "ALL- RIGHT! Okay! Let's go get this bird!"

"Naw-naw! Not just yet. He's tossing silver dollars like they were toys. I've got some more investigating to do. Let's go to the saloon. This guy is poor. He's getting this silver from somewhere. Come on, deputy," said Carson.

When the sheriff and his deputy walked into the saloon, there was Bart Winson at a gambling table. The mayor was taking his leisure at the same table.

"Hold your positions, boys. I've got some business with your sheriff," Lee Venon Rose said to the card players.

"I was wondering what would bring you to Gun-Fire Valley, Mr Mayor. Luckily, I walked in," Carson said.

"My town is a stone's throw from here. I'll be back before they miss me. Come over here to the bar. Let's talk." stated Rose.

"I understand you weren't around when the stage was almost held up. Mind telling me where you were? Judge Haney is very interested."

"Where I was, Mr. Mayor, was on an outing with Miss Weston. She'll verify that. You tell that to the honorable Judge Haney," Carson stated.

"I certainly will. Another thing. This might interest you. We're thinking about giving the town a new home," said the mayor.

"Why would that interest me?" Carson asked.

"You've been taking a lot of liberty beyond your own town. Everyone knows Sheriff Bands is a floater. We just might combine the three towns.

You'll be legal then. A bigger town, a bigger paycheck," said the mayor. "I'll keep you posted. I gotta get back to the game. The boys are getting nervous," said Lee as he started to walk away.

"You got law in each town. Where will they go? " Asked Carson.

"Bands is already restless, Billard says he's gonna move on soon. It'll work out," said Lee Venon Rose.

"One more thing, Mr. Mayor. This isn't the first time I've seen you here. You could've talked to me before, " stated Carson. "I know, " said Rose "I know. You see, ever since Doll-face Dolly got her job with the doctor, she moved out of our town temporarily. I've gotta keep up with her."

As the mayor went back to his seat, it wasn't long before Bart declared, "I fold!" He threw in his cards and started to storm out of the Saloon.

"Hold on thar, Winson!" declared the deputy. "We need a word with you!"

"Hey! I just lost my shirt! What could you want?" asked Winson angrily.

"How about some silver dollars?" asked Roy.

"I'm out! If I had money I'd still be there at the table! I'm out! Leave me alone!" screamed Winson.

"Let him go, Roy. We've got time," said Carson. "Let him go."

"Okay! Okay! Well, I guess you want more time to hassle Doll-face."

"Well, yeah," said Carson. "You could say that. Besides, he's not bluffing. He wouldn't leave a card game if he didn't have to. You know how seriously these players take card games.

"Yeah, I guess you ' re right. He'll slip up. We'll get him." said the deputy.

In Delton, Mayor Lee Venon Rose was having his problems. Sheriff Bands had moved on and Steve Wynn was appointed the new sheriff. Since Shelley Weston was very close to the family of Steve Wynn, she agreed to be his deputy. The job carried much danger with lawless men like the Sherley brothers. Bart Winson had become friends with the Sherleys, so Kirby Carson took his time about harassing him. Carson knew that time was on his side and since Winson lived in Delton, a few miles away, he was in Steve Wynn's jurisdiction.

Mayor Rose and his committee were in the process of changing the name of the town from Delton to Ridgepoint. The mayor also seemed to be losing his hold on Dolly 'Doll-Face' James and Charley (Top-gun) Judson had his eye on her, but she had been seen hanging on the arm of bad boy Spud Dawson, Ted Dawson's twin brother. True enough Dolly James was a free spirit with her flirting, but she was no easy prey or pick up. She was Dr. Walter W. Waller's nurse and was very professional at her job. Although she was seen with her share of admirers, she was surprisingly virtuous, and the doctor was very protective of her.

Her choice of men varied from clean cut to borderline bad boys. She sometimes decided to live dangerously by teasing and flirting with the likes of Charley (Top Gun) Judson, a fierce killer. A few weeks later would prove this. Judson's low profiling was to end.

In Gunbelt, the Porter brothers were trying to spread their fear to the other towns. With King Thompus yet incarcerated, it was their place to make sure their uncle still ran things, and none was trying to take over.

Paul Billard was yet keeping order with Rin Delton as his deputy. Billard had had his troubles with Pete Briggs and the Porters. He had lost a fight with Briggs, but when he out punched Vince Porter, he was aware he needed help. They wanted to gang up on him so drawing his six gun as quick as they had seen a man whip out a six gun, they held their peace. Billard then sent for Delton.

The townspeople knew well of Delton's reputation but knew nothing of the fact that he and Billard were two of a kind. They had to keep trouble from brewing in Jess March's saloon (called 'Hardy's') as well as keeping the town streets. This was not an easy thing to accomplish with men like Charley Judson and his henchmen in the next town and not letting anyone forget it. The Porter boys and Bart Winson kept their guns ready for the Sherley brothers.

Steve Wynn, Billard, and Kirby Carson were the lawmen of the three lawless towns. The gunmen held a certain degree of respect for these three. Carson was good with his guns, but he was no gunfighter. He felt that in due time, the gunslingers would wipe themselves out. Whatever it took to keep law and order and keep yourself safe while doing it was the objective. Sheriff Bands' reason for being so restless and moving on had to do with rumors that the men he wanted revenge on were seen in other areas. The faithful followers called, the Nevada group, would follow wherever he led. On occasion Bands would return to continue his fight against lawlessness.

Jesse March not only ran the Gunbelt saloon called 'Hardy's,' but he had his own group of henchmen. The Porters and Big Pete Briggs were his main guns. Standing in for King Thompus was right up his way of thinking. He considered himself chief of the lot with Thompus' nephews at his command. All the outlaws realized that King Thompus had organized a safe haven for men whose path had gone afoul of law and order.

While the three towns grew rapidly without his presence, Angus Thompus, alias ex-king Thompus, was biding his time in prison. Regular visits by his nephews, the Porter brothers and Gerry Winson kept him informed on how things were progressing. A black minister who had been a missionary on horseback was pastoring a church between the two towns. Indians from each side of the Gun-Fire Valley Mountain range would attend the church services along with the various settlers and newcomers. They experienced no trouble from either town for there was no reason to trouble churches. A certain respect was upheld.

"It's a fact," Ex-king Thompus said to the inmates that surrounded him in the large prison courtyard, "when I was on the outside, I attended every church service that I could; some called it hypocrisy."

"Well, was it?" asked one of the listeners. "You seemed to have gotten most of your wealth by hook or crook."

"You got a lot of guys makin' a statement like that to me. You know what a powerful man I am." said Thompus.

"You run things on the other side of the walls, Thompus. You're inside with us. You've been dethroned," the inmate said.

"Well!" stated Thompus. "Well, anyway, my attending church was no preference. I think we all need to know our afterlife destiny. My time to rule anything can go like a vapor."

"Yeah, Thompus," said another. "Preach to us. Maybe some of us would rather hear it from a man who hasn't done all the things you've done. Not every man in church has the church in him."

"And…" added another, "some of us would like to hear it from you, Thompus, provided you are somewhat repentant."

"It's good to know a man can come to repentance after running a ragged life, "another spoke up. "You see that big, black guy over there leanin' against the wall lookin' this way?"

"Yeah," said Thompus. "That's 'Hot-Shot' Robinson."

"Anyway," the inmate continued, "he killed two men and laid them on the railroad tracks so the train could get rid of the evidence. When he got out, he got into it with his old man. The old man had to take a hatchet to him to get him off him. Naturally, he wound up right back here. Yes, even ole hot shot can repent."

"Yeah, well, anyway," Thompus said, "my sources tell me that one of the towns started law and then the other. Now all three are watchin' the gunmen. The whole place could stand repentin'"

"By the way, Thompus," one of the inmates interrupted, "I hear one of your boys on the other side of this camp is about to be released...Johnny 'Sweetshot' Logan, by name."

"Yeah, I hear," said Thompus. "He was up for attempted murder. They really could've gotten him for other things. We won't go into all that, though. A fella could incriminate himself by talking too much."

"Yeah, Thompus," said an inmate. "You sound quite repentant to me. You certainly get my vote."

"When that new preacher came to town," said Thompus, "he wasn't alone. He had a couple of well armed buddies to assure his safety. One of them was a sure 'nough gunfighter they say. That preacher had more than angels on his side. More than angels."

"If he is true to the words he preaches," one man spoke up and said, "then he really wouldn't need those gunmen. No sir! The angels would be plenty."

"I totally agree," Thompus answered. "I reckon if it wasn't for angels, Judge "Hang 'em" Haney would've hung more than my hat. I understand too well."

One of the inmates asked, "Thompus, when you get out of here, will it be business as usual, or since you seemed to be somewhat of a changed man, will you kinda---errr--you know--uh, go straight?"

"I'll make as many amends as I can," Thompus replied. "Ben Masters would be proud to hear of it."

Back in Gun-Fire Valley, Kirby Carson is making a move to solve the bank robbery as well the attempted stagecoach hold-up. Riding to the Rum farm, he is met by Shelley Weston on the trail.

"Whoa, Coney," he said to his palomino as the two riders met each other. "Hey my dollin', "he said to Shelley. "Where're you headin'?"

"Dollin'?" She asked.

"Yeah" he said. "That's a cross between the living doll that you are and the "darling" that you are."

"Oh," she said. "That's cute." Carson leaned over and gave Midnight a couple of pats.

Shelley sighed, "I still don't understand how Midnight took to you since he seemed so--uh, shy of every other man, or 'cautious' might be a better word. He really seems to have taken to you."

"Well maybe he got that from you," stated Carson with a slight smile.

"You really mistreated my animal," she said to Carson.

"What?" he asked. "In what way?"

"I brush him down every day. I came out the next morning and I find him sweaty. I've had Dr. Waller check him over thinking he might be sick or something."

"Oh yeah," said Carson. "I truly apologize for that. I did ride him hard and didn't have time to brush him down afterward. For that I apologize to the both of you."

"Your mystery riding gave him exercise, but I'm sure he wasn't used to being put away wet." Shelley stated.

"So" said Carson, "Where did you say you were headin?"

"Back to work. I'm a deputy sheriff. You know Steve is expecting me."

"Yeah, Tin-star. I guess Dawson is too."

"Ted--yes, I'd say he is. He's considering taking my place as deputy. He doesn't want me on this job."

"I can't blame him. I'm about to embark on tugging on the criminal element myself."

"Oh? What are you about?" she asked.

"I'm going after Bart Winson...and the Sherley brothers." Carson said.

"Oh!" said Shelley. "That is dangerous. Please, Kirby---please be careful. Maybe---maybe you should wait."

"Wait?" Asked Carson. "Wait for what?"

"Well," Shelley said slowly, "Bart lives in Gunbelt, and the Sherley Brothers live in Delton-or Ridgepoint now that the name has changed. Why don't I talk to Steve and maybe we can help in some way since the Sherleys are in our town."

"Those guys are fierce," said Carson. "Maybe waiting isn't a bad idea. Perhaps I can send for Ben Masters."

"Ben is a U.S. Marshall," said Shelley... "and maybe Bands will be back. You can use his help with those gunmen. Are you sure you have enough on Bart to go after him?'

"I think so. Of course, I would have to wait for him to come to Gun-Fire Valley," said Carson. "He'll be back. As long as Dolly James works for Doc Waller he'll be back."

"Yes, Kirby," Shelley said. "You guys like that girl's straight, blonde hair and her pretty face. Yes, I am sure you're right. He'll be back."

"You like blonde hair yourself," smiled Carson. "Those Dawson twins have turned a few heads."

"It's not just Ted's blonde hair" said Shelley as she smiled and lowered her head. "He's sweet. He well, he--`

"So, what's wrong with my black hair?" asked Carson.

"Nothing," said Shelley. "Nothing at all."

"And nothing's wrong with your dark, brown hair," said Carson.

"So, what happened to us?"

"Well, nothing, "said Shelley. "I----nothing. Well, Ted happened. Ted...but I still have feelings for you...but, I... I guess I love him."

"Well," said Carson. "Well, I guess that's direct enough." Turning Coney's reigns, Carson rode away.

"Oh!" she thought as she watched him ride away. "I've hurt him. I'm so sorry. He might just go and take on those killers."

Carson changed his mind about going to the Rum farm and headed for the Indian camp. Arriving there he was met by six Indian braves.

"It's Man-kirs," one of them said.

"Go and tell Big Mountain." As one brave rode off, Carson saluted the other five.

"I'm looking for Two-Feather and Little Horse. Have you seen them?"

"They soon arrive. Been on hunting trip. Soon to return," one of the braves answered.

"I will go and talk with Chief Montus," Carson said, and he rode on to meet the chief. "We will pow-wow until the trackers come."

When the hunting party returned with their slain prey, Carson asked the two trackers to take him to where the bank-robbers had hidden the bank money.

After knowing where the money had been hidden, Carson discovered that there was more stolen money besides the bank's money.

"Looks like these guys have been at it for quite some time," thought Carson. "No wonder they always have stakes for betting."

After this discovery, Carson thanked the braves and rode back to Gun-Fire Valley. "We'll get these guys at the right time."

Arriving at the jail, Carson greeted his deputy. "Hey, Roy Slim. Hey, I've got a question. You never told me your real name. I know it can't be 'Slim'".

"You're right Kirby," stated Roy. "My last name is so hard for people to pronounce properly, so I never bother to even expose it. You can just keep on calling me "Roy Slim" just like always."

"Okay, Roy Slim," said Carson. "Tomorrow, I'll take you to where the bank loot is hidden. We'll have to make sure the Sherley brothers don't see us."

"You know where it is?" Roy asked excitedly.

"You'll be amazed how much is there, man." Carson said." These fellows have been in business for quite some time. We'll set our trap for those guys, but I plan to get Bart Winson first."

"Yeah, Winson," said Roy. "Hey, what's with that guy? He came to town buddying with the Sherley boys and now he's with the Porter brothers--devout enemies."

"'Yeah" said Carson. "I heard that. He's traded the devil for the witch."

"Wow!" said Roy, "some trade."

"Well, we'll wait for him to come to town. No sense in going out of our jurisdiction when he can't seem to stay away from Dolly."

"Dolly lives in Ridgepoint--or Delton--or whatever the name is this week," said Roy. "Yeah, but she doesn't miss any work at Doc Waller's. We've got time."

In Ridgepoint, Shelley Weston told Sheriff Steve Wynn of Carson's plan to go after Bart Winson and the Sherleys. Wynn agreed with Shelley that they would keep an eye on the brothers in case Carson made a move. Shelley felt that Carson might get too careless with his life after their last conversation. She wanted to help him as much as she could.

A few days later, Kirby Carson waited outside Dr. Waller's office for Dolly James to go out for lunch.

"Hello, Tin-star," she said as she stepped out of the building.

"How have you been?"

"My luck is down," said Carson as the two started walking. "I haven't seen Winson for a while. What rock is he hiding under?"

"Maybe you should ask Gerry Winson. You like to talk to nice-looking women, don't you?" said Dolly. "She doesn't like lawmen, I hear."

"She's his sister, right?" asked Carson.

"You know she is. You also know she's pretty," said Dolly.

"Are you saying you haven't seen Bart?" Carson asked.

"Not lately. He hangs with the Porter bunch," she said. "They are practically his brothers, you know. I mean, she is their adopted sister. That's why he had to cut the Sherley boys loose."

"Yeah, that makes sense," Carson said. "That makes a lot of sense. Hmmm! But still, you mean he isn't on your trail anymore?"

"I think he got nervous when Charley Judson made some kind of remark about my being something sweet for his eyes," Dolly said and smiled.

"Judson! Top Gun! Dolly, you---you---you need to be careful--" Carson said rather excitedly.

"I am careful," Dolly said, "I am. I know how far to take my flirting. I'm careful. Don't worry."

"You catch a lot of eyes Doll face. One man might have trouble holding onto you," said Carson.

"Oh, no," said Dolly. "Once I choose my man I settle down. My flirting ceases. Any admirers I might have will have to give it up."

"You are worth fighting for. Should I.... or maybe I should stake my claim," Carson said.

"You have a roving heart, Tin-star," she said. "How would I be able to trust you?"

"I'm trustworthy all right," Carson said. "My heart can settle down."

"Sure, it can, Tin-star. Sure, it can," Dolly said.

"Well, I can't wait for Bart forever. I promised Roy, I would show him some proof a couple days ago. I'll see you around," Carson said as he walked back to the jail.

As Carson and Roy Slim mounted up and headed out of town, they discussed what manner of plan they would use to finally trap Bart Winson. With no stolen money to tie him to, it would take trickery to make a conviction stick. They would not have that problem with the Sherleys. Making sure they were not followed by the Sherleys, they were met with another surprise. As they approached the hiding place, they heard hoof-beats. Dodging quickly behind some large boulders, they were out of sight when a lone rider rode by.

"Hey" said Roy, "that---that's Paul--Paul Billard."

"And he's coming from the hiding place," said Carson. "Come on. Let's have a look."

"Look at what?" Roy asked, as they rode a dozen yards more and dismounted.

"You'll see," said Carson. "Gotta see if anything has been disturbed. If you didn't know this cave was here, you'd never find it."

"Wow!" said Roy. "You're absolutely right!"

Carson and Roy slipped between the two large boulders that led to a cave well hidden, behind some bushes, they entered into the hiding place of outlaw's treasure.

"There are candles and a couple of lamps in here. Home, sweet home" said Carson as he put fire to the first candle. As the two lawmen continued to light up the cave, they checked out the bank's money and three other containers of stolen loot.

"My stars," said Roy. "How high will these guys hang when we trap them. Great time O' day!"

"I was thinking, Roy," said Carson. "Since these monies aren't together, one group of robbers just may not know about the other. Did you notice how one stack is concealed pretty good behind these piles of rock and the other is placed on this ledge against the wall?"

"Hmmm" thought Roy. "One robber might not know about the other and... but the lamps and candles..."

"The first guy, or whoever, probably hid his loot first, not having much lighting. The next group had no idea that the first guy had even been here, "said Carson.

"So maybe Billard was the first guy, huh? Or why else would he be coming out of this area?"

"I doubt if he was just passing by. I'm sure he isn't on a venture trying to trap a robber," smiled Carson.

"Yeah" said Roy. "That's our job."

"Let's get out of here," said Carson. "We don't want the bad guys to catch us here. Blow out these candles."

"This area is close to the place they call the "edge" where those wolves hang around," said Roy. "I wouldn't want to be out here at night."

"Yea" said Carson. "They really come out after dark. Some of the Indians watch a pack of these wolves attack a cougar who had killed a deer."

"I Guess the cougar was too outnumbered." Roy said.

"They said it was quite a battle, but he who is hungrier fights the hardest. The cat had to give it up, though. That wolf pack was far too much for the cougar," said Carson. "The last time I was near the 'edge', those wolves were tearing into a horse."

"It would sure be nice if we knew what Billard is up to," said Roy as the two rode back to town.

"Yeah," thought Carson, thinking out loud, "It'd be quite funny if we have to watch a sheriff as well some outlaws. What we need is a spy. Hmmm! Maybe an Indian. Huh? The loot behind the rocks had not been touched for quite some time. Maybe months or longer. Maybe Billard was mainly checking on that."

"Interesting'," said Roy.

"Interesting. Very," said Carson. "Very."

"You seem pretty steel-minded sure that Billard is the guy who stored the first loot, Kirb! What are you basing this on?"

"It's been rumored around that Billard is really Paul Bolton, the last of the brothers that never got caught." Carson continued, "Those guys were killers. I've been putting various clues together ever since I heard that. You heard that 'where there's smoke, there's fire.' Some rumors are just rumors. Some pan out to be facts. Those brothers evidently hid the first loot years ago. Billard would be making sure it's still safe. He came back to this wild country for something. I figure it's the money. At the right time, I figure he plan to grab it and leave for good. For one reason or another, he's still here."

"I figure," said Roy, "if you're right about this guy, he's probably trying to see who else has put loot in his hide-out. If he's still looking, that might keep him here. The Sherley boys don't seem to be aware that Billard's loot is even there."

"That could be it," said Carson. "Time will tell if we could catch them there together. I guess only circumstances would present this. With these bad wolves of the Edge on the prowl, not too many people like this area."

Two days later, Bart Winson rode into Gun-Fire Valley.

☙∞❧

As Carson and Roy Slim walked into the saloon, there they found him at a gambling table.

"Bart Winson," said Carson, "you're under arrest."

"What?" asked Winson, "When is it a law for a man to play a game of poker? I am on a wining-streak here."

"Well maybe you'll win your case in court! Let's go," said Carson.

As Dr. Waller looked from his window, he saw the two lawmen taking Winson to jail. "Hey, Dolly," said the doctor, "Come, look. I see Carson finally caught Bart Winson for one thing or another."

"Yes," said Dolly James." I let Kirby know that Bart was in town. He's been waiting on him for a while."

"I know Winson's a rebel-rouser. I wonder what Carson's got him on.

"I wonder if he'll be able to prove anything. I could be implemented. Bart did borrow my horse once."

"Once?" asked Waller. "What could he have done with your mane on a one-time trip?"

"I don't know" Dolly said, turning away. "Maybe nothing. Nothing at all."

"What---wait a minute. That failed stagecoach hold-up. That shoulder wound. Dolly---well, we'll see," said Dr. Waller. "We are both innocent you know. We'll see, Dolly. We'll see."

⌘

At the jail, Bart Winson is protesting. "Why in the world am I here lawman? You can't prove I had anything to do with that stagecoach. Prove it, I say! Prove it!"

"We'll prove it in court," said Carson. "Judge Haney will be here in two days. We'll prove it all right, we'll prove it."

Two days later court was in session. Judge Thomas Thornton Haney presided. Six cases were on the docket. "Hang 'em" Haney had a full day since other judges from various areas had sent some of their cases to him because their own dockets were overloaded.

Dr. W.W. Waller and nurse Dolly James took a front row seat. Mayor Lee Venon Rose rode in from Ridgepoint to attend the event. People from the three towns were present. Judge Haney's court only took place on certain occasions. Other magistrates usually handled most local cases.

When Bart Winson's name was called, his sister Gerry and Paul Billard stood up. Billard, because he was sheriff of Winson's area. Gerry, because it was her brother. When they both sat down, the statements were heard.

"You are charged with attempted robbery of a stagecoach. How do you plead?" One of the Porter brothers was studying law.

"Your honor, I'm Louis Porter, attorney. I represent Bart Winson. We plead "Not guilty!""

As the court moved a long, sheriff Carson acted as prosecutor.

"This man was seen by witnesses during and after the action at hand."

"That's a lie" exploded Porter. "That masked rider could've been anybody! I heard it could've even been you sheriff."

"Order! Order in the court!" called Haney, banging his gavel. "I will have no outbursts!"

As the arguments continued, the judge finally asked for Carson's witnesses. Carson called Dr. Walter Walter Waller. After Dr. Waller told of digging a bullet out of Winson's shoulder, the judge had to agree with Louis Porter that Winson could have gotten shot at any time or in any of the lawless towns. This evidence would not stand.

"Have you any other witnesses, sheriff?" asked Judge Haney.

"Yes", answered the sheriff. "I call four braves from chief Flaming Eagle's tribe. Bold Arrow will speak for the group."

As the brave, Bold Arrow, was being sworn in, his chief stood up attentively.

"We watch the road much. Each day we watch, "stated Bold Arrow. As he told what he and the others observed, Porter objected.

"I object! Your honor, I object!" This man could hang for this! Are you going to take the word of an Injun'? I object!"

"Overruled! Sit down!" ordered the judge. Please continue."

"We follow wounded man. He remove mask. We follow him to town. This is the man "stated Bold Arrow.

After the witness was excused, the judge asked Carson, "Why did you take so long to arrest this man if you knew all this?"

"Well," said Carson, "I... I

was waiting for you to make your rounds this way. Besides, Winson is out of my jurisdiction. I had to wait for him to come back to Gun-Fire Valley."

"Hold the prisoner while I deliberate." said the judge. "I will make my determination in a few days. I will see the attorney and prosecutor in my chambers and let them know when I will rule."

As Bart Winson was returned to the jail cell, his sister Gerry followed. Roy Slim watched Paul Billard. Billard mounted up and rode away. Dolly and Dr. W. W. Waller walked back to this office. Dolly noticed Mayor Rose and told the doctor, "I'll see you later. I must talk to Lee."

"Lee huh?" asked the doctor.

"Lee", repeated Dolly.

After catching up with Rose, Dolly asked him, "Can't you do anything to help Bart? I mean, can they really hang him for this? I mean really--it was an attempted hold up- not a real hold-up. Can you, Mr. Mayor?"

"I don't see what I can do, Dolly. I mean attempted is just as bad as the real thing," the mayor said. "If I were a governor, I could no doubt give him a pardon. I'm only a mayor."

"But isn't there something you can do?" asked Dolly. "Something at all?

"You--you like this guy, don't you?" asked Rose.

"Well, 'like'... yeah," said Dolly. "I do like him, He's---he's interesting. I don't want to see him hanged."

"Well maybe he'll just get some time," said Rose.

"Time?" asked Dolly, "He's standing before "Hang em" Haney! King Thompus the Hat is still hanging in the judge's courthouse!"

"Well, that's just a nickname. Though I admit he has hung over his share of wrong doers." said Rose.

"Well, I'm not willing to gamble on a nickname, Lee."

"Well, what? What do you want of me?" asked Rose.

"You're adventurous! You're creative. Please Lee. Think of something." said Dolly.

"Okay," said Rose. "Come to my office after work and I'll see what I can come up with."

After a visit with her brother, Gerry Winson decided to look up Judge Haney. The big man was not hard to find. He stood six feet and was well overweight. Gerry located him in the saloon, standing at the bar.

"What'll you have your honor? It's on me" she said.

"I just had two cups of coffee, lady. Thank you. I've had enough."

"What's going to become of my brother?" she asked.

"Attempted robbery", he said. "What would you say if you to make the call?"

"Oh, I guess I might say; 'thirty days bread and water. I could be lenient, your honor."

"I suppose you could. I'm afraid the call just isn't yours to make, my lady."

"But you could be, sir. It was only attempted," Gerry said pleadingly.

"That's all I can say about the case my lady," said the judge and he tipped his hat and departed.

"Cold" thought Gerry. "This man is cold. Bart doesn't stand a chance. I have to see what Louis has to say about Bart's chances.' With this, Gerry also departed.

Gerry Winson returned to the jail to console her brother. Kirby Carson told Roy Slim, "Hold things down here. I've got to put a hot plan into action."

As Carson started to leave, Louis Porter came in asking to see Bart Winson. "Sure", said Carson. "Your sister is already back there."

As Carson walked out of the jail, he thought, "this is working out better than I expected. I'd better hurry."

Rushing to find the judge, Carson found him in the courthouse chambers talking with Paul Billard.

"Excuse me, your honor, but I've got a plan that will clear all doubts. Could you two come to the jail with me?"

The judge and Billard agreed and headed hurriedly to the jail. When they arrived there Carson instructed Judge Haney and Billard to stand outside of the jail window and listen. They could hear the Winsons and Louis Porter talking inside.

"I don't know about this," Judge Haney said to Carson. "I don't need this…"

Carson quieted him and asked him to just wait and listen. Leaving the two near the outside window, Carson slipped into the jail.

"We've got the goods on you, Winson." Carson said as he entered the cell area holding a stolen container of stagecoach money.

"We recovered the evidence." The Winsons looked at each other and then at Bart.

"What? What?" exclaimed Bart. "What kind of trickery is this?"

"It's the evidence," said Carson, "and you know where you had it hidden. While the judge is deliberating, I'm gonna present this."

"You---you're crazy! I didn't even--" Bart was saying when he was interrupted by Porter.

"Wait a minute, Bart!" Porter said. "Don't say anything--"

"But I didn't even get anything from that stagecoach--- I"

"You got shot before you could rob the stage," Carson stated. "Is that what you're saying?"

Carson stepped to the window and asked, "you fellows heard enough?"

"We've heard enough, sheriff," the judge answered. Gerry Winson ran to the window and began cursing as she watched Judge Haney and Paul Billard walking away.

"Easy, Baby," Louis said, comforting Gerry. "This isn't over yet."

As the judge entered the jail, he asked, "Where'd you get the money, Carson?"

"Let's just say I borrowed it from the stage line. My deputy knows about it," Carson said. "The main point is this is the man who tried to rob the stage."

"Like I said," Louis Porter stated as he and Gerry Winson were leaving the jail, "this isn't over!" Then glaring at Carson, Louis said "and you sheriff---you! Getting those redskins to testify! You knew the judge wasn't going to insult those Indians with their chief standing there."

With this, Porter stormed out of the building. "If this man is Karrah-Vanno, then he has a lot more than attempted robbery to answer for," Roy Slim said to the judge.

"I'm dealing with the attempted robbery right now men," said Judge Haney as he turned and walked out.

"I heard that deputy!" cried Bart from his jail cell. "I heard that! You guys won't be satisfied until I'm swinging!"

"Relax," called Carson. "You also heard the judge; everyone knows there's more than one Karrah-Vanno."

"They're piling more stuff on me than--I'll never get out of all this--" murmured Bart.

"I'll be back Roy, "said Carson to his deputy. "I gotta turn this money back."

"I Don't know if that was a smart move or not, Kirb," said Roy.

"Don't sweat it Roy," said Carson. "It worked, didn't it?"

As evening was falling, Carson was yet away delivering the stage line money. The managers were quite amazed to see stolen money returned and undisturbed.

"It's been a while when this money was taken," the manager said.

"Our coverage took care of it--this is good! This is good!" I guess the robber was waiting a while before trying to spend it. That would be wise.

"I suppose," answered Carson. "I suppose. He had it tucked away at a boarding house. We were lucky to recover it."

"We were lucky," said the manager. "Yes! We were lucky! Thanks sheriff. Thanks a lot." Carson then rode back for Gun-Fire Valley.

When Carson returned, he decided to ride on to the Rum farm. Little did he realize what was going on back at the jail.

As Roy Slim was eating his late supper that had been delivered to the jail, a masked black arrayed man came through the door with gun in hand. "Get the keys and head for the cell Deputy," the muffled voice demanded.

"You can finish your supper in the lock up." Roy grabbed the keys and his plate of food and headed for the second cell. The masked man relieved him of his six gun and locked him in.

"Come on" the masked man said to Bart Winson as he unlocked his cell.

"Who are you?" Winson asked. "I'm not sure I want to go with you." Was that You?

"Would you rather hang?" asked the masked man.

"No! No, not at all," said Bart as he hurriedly left the cell.

When Carson arrived at the jail, he found Roy Slim locked in the jail cell sound asleep. "Now, wait a minute," Carson said. "What Roy? What in the world is going on around here?"

"Don't even ask" Roy said. "Karrah-Vanno? Would you believe? Karrah-Vanno? Huh? Great time o'day!"

"Okay! Okay! Where's the keys?" asked Carson.

"I don't know, Kirby," Roy said. "Look around." Carson found the keys lying on the floor. Unlocking the cell for Roy, Carson had noticed the empty plate.

"What'd you have for supper?" Carson smiled and asked.

"What about Bart Winson? What will the judge say now? That wasn't you that let him out. This guy was not as tall as you."

"I didn't think the Porters would stoop to a thing like this," Carson said.

"I don't think it was any of the Porters," Roy stated. "This guy was different. No, it was not one of them. Smooth- this guy was smooth."

"Well, it wasn't me. My Karrah-Vanno days are over." Carson said.

The next day the news headline read: "Caravano strikes Again!"

The editor of the 'News Letter' admitted, "I only heard the name. How would I know how to spell it?"

"You spelled it the way it sounds," said one of the readers.

"Caravano". How would the Indians spell it?"

"They wouldn't. They just say it." another said.

The same day found Louis Porter at the territorial prison visiting ex-king Thompus, his uncle. The news of Bart Winson's escape had reached Thompus before Porter even got there. Louis Porter was not even aware that Winson was no longer in jail. "What?" he asked, "Who? What happened? Did you...did you pull some strings- I mean, I was going to see if you could---"

"No, no" said Thompus. "I haven't done a thing. I can't see what I could've done anyway. When I got word of his trial, I racked my brain for an answer in case worse comes to worst."

"But-but if he is caught, will he hang?" asked Porter.

"Attempted robbery? Naw--he would no doubt get some time, I'm sure, but escaping jail might change all that. It could go hard on him if he's caught."

"If he turned himself in?" asked Porter. "That would help, I guess," Thompus answered. "What kind of guy is Bart? Will he even have a mind to do that?"

"Turn himself in?" asked Porter. "It's hard to read that guy. I don't know if he will or no."

As Carson and his deputy sat on the porch of the jail, Gerry Winson rode up to the jail and dismounted. "You realize your brother isn't here, don't you?" Carson asked.

"Yes, sheriff," she answered, "I'm aware that my brother isn't here, no thanks to you."

"Then what can we possibly do for you, ma'am? We're at your disposal," Carson said.

"I wonder if I can have Bart's gun belt and his gun?" she asked.

Carson looked at Roy and then back at Gerry.

"Well, I suppose so ma'am" he said, "You know I watch you use those colts each fourth of July. Is your brother as good as you?"

At this, she whipped out both colts and fired at a nearby tree.

"I've gotten better sheriff. You won't have to wait for the fourth."

"Wow" said Roy as he stepped over to see the tree. "Those slugs are less than an inch apart."

"I guess that answers my question. If he was close to being that good, we would have known it." Carson said.

"May I please, now have his things?!" she said.

"Of course, ma'am," he said. "I don't suppose you'll be taking them to him."

"Why don't you just follow me and see, sheriff? You might not come back."

"Now why would you say such a thing to me?" he asked.

"I just decided to be honest with you sheriff, I think I dislike you as much as I dislike Paul Billard."

"You don't like Billard?" Carson asked.

"I hate him. He knows it. Now you do." she answered as she mounted up and rode away.

"What a beautiful blonde enemy," Carson said as he watched her ride off.

"Real smooth," said Roy. "Blondes, brunettes, any color hair, huh Kirb?"

"Hey, Roy, I was thinking" Carson said as he turned to Roy, "Speaking of smooth, who would you say is the smoothest dancer at the hall?"

"Well, er, you're pretty good. Then there's other guys like--well, if Sweetshot Logan was here, he would be about the best, I guess, why?"

"Yeah, but who would you say would be considered 'smooth'?"

"Uh---the mayor! Yeah! Lee Venon Rose. There's no smoother dancer in the three towns that L. Venon Rose. You agree?"

"I certainly do. Now, think about it, think back. How did you describe that masked jail-breaker guy?"

"Rose! He was just the right size!" said Roy.

"What tipped you to Rose, Kirb?" Roy asked.

"Well, as I said," Carson answered, "I was thinking----you mentioned the man was smooth. He is so cool with it that he's smooth in about everything he does. It's his makeup. He's got to be the masked man."

"Alright" said Roy. "How do we trap him?"

"The mayor? Naw! Let's ride with it for now. We have to figure out why he would be involved okay. He likes Dolly, Dolly kinda like Bart-- hmm! Okay, let's say he did it for her. That's a tall order. He'd be risking everything. But for Dolly, I guess he might" Carson said.

"She could probably talk me into it, you think?"

"I think any of those gals could," said Roy. "Shelley Weston, Gerry Winson--even if she hates lawmen, Miss March, Miss Linder, those school teachers, you know you would."

Meanwhile, in Ridgepoint, Lee Venon Rose was holding on to Dolly James's hand as she is saying, "Now Lee, you know I am late for work. I am always on time; the doctor will think something has happened to me and he'll worry."

"As I said, my lovely," Rose said to Dolly, "I took a WHALE of a chance for you. You gave me your word you would be mine. I just need to say some things to you as well."

"You know me as a straight, off-the-cuff mayor of this town, a slick, fast dealing gambler, champion on the dance floor, and as you said, creative adventurous and now, as the newspaper said- 'Caravano'! Now I say this to you, my lovely. If you will give yourself to me totally, heart and soul, I will always be L. Venon Rose, the man you see before you. No fast-dealing guy you can't trust, no silver-tongued slickster, whatever you want, baby. I'll even take up farming or even ranching--whatever turns your crank. That'll be me, whatever you want me to be."

"You are sweet Lee," Dolly said. "You don't have to change. What you are is what drew me to you. But, really, Darling," she continued, "I must go to work. By the way, you really played the part, riding my black mare and pulling off that escape. I knew you would think of something."

As Dolly departed, Rose was thinking of what a fool hearty plan he was able to pull off. *"It's a good thing the sheriff wasn't there. There could've been gunplay. I'm good, but Carson's better. What a chance--what chance I took for the company of Dolly (Doll-face) James. I guess I'd do whatever it takes to have her. That Dawson kid wants her, Top gun Judson--wow! Top-gun Judson- I guess I am living dangerously. Well, she's worth it. I'll take my chances."*

Johnny 'Sweetshot' Logan was being released from the territorial prison. He too has eyes for Dolly.

In Gun-Fire Valley, Kirby Carson was coming out of the jail's office when two of Chief Montus' braves rode up.

"Man-Kirs," they saluted the sheriff, "Come quickly. Our father calls for you. Him plenty sick. Calls for Man-Kirs."

As Carson put his foot in one of Cony's stirrups, another rider came up on a palomino.

"Hold it, men," said Carson. "That looks like…it is. It's Sheriff Bands. Howdy, Pod-nah!"

"Hey there, Carson" replied Bands. "Where you off to?"

"Indian camp…Chief Montus…I'm in a hurry." stated Carson settle in on Cony.

"Mind if I ride along? I'll explain on the way." said Bands.

"Let's ride." said Carson. "Hold the fort, Roy!"

"I got it." said Roy Slim tipping his hat.

As Carson, Bands, and the braves rode on, Bands had some exciting news to share with Carson.

"The Nevada boys and I caught up with two of the men I've been after. There were three of them. Two young guys and an old man and two of them open fire on us. They wounded two of our men. We killed one of 'em. We shot the other man, but he got away. The dying man apologized for being one of the men who killed my brother. Before he died, he said the older man was hiding among the Indians. He said it was near here."

"Hmmm" thought Carson, "you couldn't have come at a better time. This might just be your man."

"Huh? What do you mean, Carson?" Bands asked with a curious look on his face.

As Carson explained his mission and that of the two Indian Braves, one of the Braves asked, "Is this the man you were to give the message to?"

"Yes, this is the man. If the White Father is still alive, I reckon he can give it to him in person." said Carson.

When the riders reached the Indian camp, they were led to Chief Montus' tent where the old man that had become the Chief's blood-brother lay dying.

After the various salutes, the old man looked up surprisingly and stated, "Bands! I didn't expect to see you, I'm dying. I'm glad you're here. I was going to send a word to you. That crazy nephew of mine did the shooting. I know! I'm just as guilty. That's why we all ran. I want to make my peace with you." Sheriff Bands stood quietly and listened. The old man continued, struggling to get his words out he said, "My nephew, my brother's son, that wild spirit of his couldn't be tamed."

"Well, we got one of 'em," Bands said, "He told us about where we might find you."

"I know. My nephew was here. He said you got Fletch. He was a wild one. You got him pretty good, too, but the Indians wouldn't let him stay. He went too far with one of the maidens when we all were accepted in by the chief here," the old man said catching his breath, "and the Indians kicked him out."

"You say we got him good--where did he go?" asked Bands.

"Out toward the Edge. He's hit pretty bad. He might be lying out there now. I don't think he can get too far. He was lucky to make it here." The old man said as his words grew softer. "I---I'm a dying man, Bands---I-I wanted to make my---peace..."

"His spirit has flown to the wind" Chief Montus stated. "His hope was to be buried. We go to new church-colored brother make us welcome."

"Well," said Carson, "Very well, I reckon. Shall we look around the Edge?" he said as he and Bands walked out. "It's night; it's dark. maybe at daylight. I've ridden a long way, but I couldn't rest until I--well, if I hadn't run into you, I would have had to wait 'til morning anyways." said Bands.

"Nighttime is no time to be anywhere near the Edge. Those crazy wolves will eat anything." said Carson.

"Well, maybe they'll get the last of the men I've been after. I hear they're a real death-pack. If he's bleeding, and I'm sure he is, I wouldn't give too much for his chances." said Bands.

The next morning Sheriff Bands was sound asleep for he had had quite a day the day before. He woke up at noon in a hotel room in Ridgepoint in time to see the noonday stagecoach arrive. As he peered from the window, he watched Johnny Sweetshot Logan step down from the stagecoach.

Logan registered at the desk to get a room. After resting and then getting himself refreshed, he set out to look for Dolly. He walked into the saloon he once operated. The regular were seated in their usual seats having their daily dose of whatever they preferred. After conversing with the bartender and others he was familiar with, Logan inquired about Dolly. Hearing the name Dolly peaked Spud Dawson interest, so he walked over and leaning on the bar asked "Why are you asking about Dolly? You a relative?"

Logan turned around to Spud and took a hard look at him. "No, I'm not a relative, are you?" asked Logan. "I mean, with your blonde hair and all?"

"Not a relative. I'm just a guy in line for her heart" Dawson said.

"Hmph!" grunted Logan. "Well join the party. You might need to know, I'm at the head of the line."

At this Dawson looked across the room at Charley Judson who was sitting alone at a table in the corner downing some whiskey. "Uh, yeah?" Dawson said with a smile.

"Him, too?" Logan asked the bartender who simply nodded at his question.

"None of 'em have a hold on her, though" said the bartender in a whisper to Logan, which gave him some relief.

Just then Sheriff Bands walked in and ordered beer and coffee. "What a combination!" exclaimed Dawson.

"Yeah" said Bands. "One to celebrate the other to keep me awake. I've got a dirty job ahead."

"Don't we all." said Dawson. "My brother and I have a small farm goin."

"Okay" said Bands slowly. "I've also got a funeral to attend. I'm hoping maybe two."

"Two funerals?" Logan turned and looked at Bands.

"Yeah" said Bands as he downed his coffee. "I'm hoping the guy I'm going after is already dead."

As Bands began to walk away, the bartender said raising a bottle, "Hey Sheriff, you forgot your beer."

"I know," said Bands, "drink it."

"That's strange" said Dawson with wonder in his eyes to Logan, as Bands left the saloon.

"You mind if I drink this?" Logan asked the bartender grabbing the beer.

"Go ahead," said the bartender. "I'm on duty."

Just then, five men walked in and joined Charley Judson at his table. Judson stood and began to speak "From now on, you guys are my henchmen." Then he turned around, stuck his chest out, raised his voice and said to the people in the saloon, "I'm serving notice. From now on, Charley Judson runs this town."

Then he added after his finished downing his drink, "And you can tell that to your mayor."

The five men stood beside Judson. There were different shapes and sizes and seems to have more confidence when they were around the big guy.

"Who are these guys?" Dawson asked.

"The big guy is Bill "Squint" Tonns, a farmer who would rather travel with bad company. That's Toby Bonds next to him." said Logan. "I'm not sure about the other three."

"Well, the one with two guns is Rory Gibbs- or I mean, 'Jibbs,'" said the bartender, "and everybody knows Joe Bunts. He's a coward. I don't even know why he's with 'em."

"Messenger boy," said Logan, "every group has one. The other must be Tom Jacobs and he's a bad one. I heard from prison he was coming to town. He has always traveled with Judson." Logan drank the beer and started to leave.

"Hold on Logan" called Judson. "I might be interested to know how sweetly you shoot."

"I'm not armed, Charley" Logan said. "I'm on parole anyway."

"I hear you got quite wealthy by getting some rich patients poisoned. You and the nurse made out pretty good."

"That's never been proven." Logan was getting irritated. "It could all be rumors. I don't need this stuff coming up again, I dealt with it back then Judson. Let it go."

"Maybe I will, for now Logan." said Judson with a smirk on his face.

"Top gun, huh Judson?" asked Dawson drinking the rest of his drink. "I got your top gun! Why are challenging unarmed men your habit? This man isn't wearing a gun. My own father was gunned down by you, you Slimy---" Dawson started to walk over to Judson.

"Hold it kid." Logan said as he grabbed Dawson by the arm. "Is this true?"

"Sure, it's true. Dolly told me who he is." Dawson heart was beating faster than normal. "This man wants to dig up a man's past. Well, he took my dad's cow and wouldn't pay him. He got my dad to draw and that was it, that was it."

"Is that what brought you to town, kid?" Judson inquired, reaching into his pocket, he tossed some money on the floor. "There's your cow money kid, pick it up."

Grabbing Dawson by the arm, Logan pulled him out of the saloon. "Come on kid. The time isn't right for this."

"You seem to be a decent man, Logan," said Dawson as they walked down the dirty road. "What about this poison stuff? Dolly had mentioned something in her past that related to this."

"Okay kid," said Logan with a sigh, "there were some very wealthy people that were close to our family and they wanted to leave us something.

They had no heirs and when they got deathly ill, I guess I persuaded the nurse to help them along. I know it sounds dirty, but they asked for relief."

"Johnny!" called the voice behind the two men. "Johnny Logan!" Logan turned to see Shelley Weston running up to him. She was accompanied by Sheriff Steve Wynn and Ted Dawson.

"Shelley Weston!" called Logan as he turned to receive her outstretched arms.

"It's so good to see you." As they walked and talked, he noticed she and Dawson's twin Ted were wearing badges.

"Yes Johnny," she said, "I was Steve's deputy and now Ted put on the badger to protect me."

"My brother, the law." said Spud as he checked out his twin.

"Yeah" said Ted. "Much law is needed."

"Even with men like "Tootsie" Dane and Curly Wilders gone, we need law to keep things peaceful" Shelley said. "I'm sure we can count on you to not stir up any old acquaintance Johnny."

"Hey sweets, I'm on parole. I don't want to go back there. Look! No guns." Logan raised his hands in the air to reveal a regular old belt.

"I'm sure you can get some." she said. "Now please, Johnny, no trouble."

"I feel the trouble will start with Charley Judson. He's already barking out threats to take over the town." Logan stated.

"Well, we'll just have to be on our guard for him," Steve said. "He's been quiet so far, but I hear his buddies have come to town to join him here."

In Gun-Fire Valley, Sheriff Bands caught up with Kirby Carson. "Daylight is wasting Carson." he said. "You are going with me to check out the Edge for that wounded outlaw, aren't you?"

"Sure, I guess," said Carson, "I expected you earlier."

"Well, I overslept. I reckon I was more worn out than I thought. Are you about ready?"

"Well, you're interrupting my regular routine, but I guess I can forego a few things. Hold 'er down Roy."

"Right" said Roy Slim sipping his coffee. "You fellers be careful around the Edge."

"We'd better be." Carson replied as he and Bands mounted up.

As the two lawmen rode out of town, they approached a group of Indians and the congregation from the new church established by the black minister.

"It's the funeral they are marching to," said Bands slowing his horse down, "I had intentions of going."

"Well, we might as well join them. We would be interrupting if we tried to ride thru them" Carson said. "I think the chief expects me anyway."

"Well, I guess me too," said Bands, "Maybe they won't hold too long."

As the funeral of the man known to the Indians as the White Father proceeded, it lasted much longer than the lawmen expected. The preacher preached long, the Indian ceremonies seemed to take forever, and Carson and Bands were getting very restless, but knowing it would have been rude and disrespectful to leave, they remained until it was over.

"Well," said Bands, "that was some experience. I learned a lot about the Bible as well as how the Indians do things, but it is getting dark, and we had better hurry if we're going to the Edge."

"It's not far from here," said Carson, "but maybe we had better try for it tomorrow."

"Tomorrow? Not so!" exploded Bands. "I'm going to the Edge to see if that guy's dead or still hanging on. You can go home if you want, but I'm going on."

"Well, I can't let you go alone," said Carson. "I reckon I'm with you, but we'll have to push these horses."

As they approached the area known as the Edge, they heard a couple of shots. As they drew closer, they could hear laughter as if from a man drunk with wine. It was the outlaw, crazed with pain and losing his mind. "That's him" said Bands, determined to see the last of his brother's killer end. Bands dismounted and ran for a closer look.

"Wait" cried Carson as two shots rang out. One shot grazed Carson's left side. As he fell from his mount, the two gunned outlaw shot again grazing the side of Carson's head, rendering him unconscious. Carson recovered temporarily enough to hear Bands say, "I'm hit Carson! He got me--".

Carson blacked out again and had no idea how long he had been out. When he came to himself, it was quite dark, and the dim moon was the only trace of light. His horse, Coney, was standing over him. The words wet and rough crossed his mind, something was licking his hand. He could hear wolves growling and fighting as his head cleared more and more and his vision was no longer blurry. The wolves fought fiercely among themselves as they were tearing the body of the wounded outlaw apart. Carson soon realized what was licking his hand was a wolf cub. Carson was to be their next meal if the wolves would have been able to pull Coney down. The she wolves were already slowly approaching him, eye fixed on him. The alpha males were too busy to notice the two lawmen. Bands lay on the ground dead from the bullet of the outlaw. His horse was about thirty yards away. Carson took Band's gun from his hand and with his own gun he fired wildly at the alpha wolves as he struggled to his feet. The she wolves fled, and Carson mounted Coney and rode over to Band's horse. Retrieving the horse and using all the strength he had left in him, he loaded Bands deadweight body over the saddle, mounted Cony, grabbed the reigns of both horses and slowly headed for home.

⸺⟨∞⟩⸺

When Carson opened his eyes again, he had no idea where he was.

"Good morning" the soft voice of Shelley Weston was saying.

"What -- where am I--how did I get here?" Carson sat up looking around, trying to put pieces together.

"Just lie back," she said gently pushing him back on to the pillow. "Lie back down."

"Where's Bands? How did I get here?"

"Relax" she said. "One question at a time. Sheriff Bands is dead. The Nevada group took his body. You are at the Rum farm—in your old recovery room."

"Nevada group? How long have I been out?" Carson inquired still feeling the pain of his wounds.

"Almost two days."

"I thought I heard you say before I was fully awake."

"That's right," she said. "What else did you hear me say? I did say a lot to you."

"That's all I heard," said Carson.

"Good" she said with relief. "I'm afraid I couldn't live up to all that I said."

"Wow" said Carson with a grin. "That's interesting. I wish I could've heard it."

Just then, Ted Dawson walked in. "How are ya lawman? If those Indians hadn't found you on the trail, well, your horse was bringing you, but it was a slow drag. You got more company. He gestured, "Come on in folks."

In came Roy Slim, Dolly James, Jennifer March, and Helen Linders. "Two schoolteachers, a nurse and a lawman," Carson said with a welcoming smile. "What a combination."

"Yeah," said Roy walking over to the bed, "with this kind of attention maybe I need to get banged up and wounded."

"Yeah." said Carson. "I'd say it's worth it."

Then Carson moved and noticed the wound on his left side. "Ouch!" he exclaimed. "I guess I forgot I got shot. How bad was it?"

"It's a flesh-wound," said Dolly, "it's a good thing you have a couple of love handles. The bullet passed right thru."

Just then Dr. Waller walked in. "Alright ladies" he said passing by, "let me have him."

As the ladies departed, Roy Slim and the doctor helped Carson to his feet. "A little wobbly but you seem to be okay" Dr. Waller stated after checking Carson out.

Two of the Indians came in as Carson was getting dressed. They informed him that the wolves he had shot at were dead.

"Three male wolves you kill" one of them said. "That leaves one alpha male to run the pack. The rest scatter because of shooting. We find outlaw's horse--bring him to Rum farm."

"The last thing I remember" said Carson to the men, "I managed to get Band's body up on his horse. I mounted Coney and the next thing I knew I was in this bed."

The ladies sat in another room as Shelley Weston was telling the others her feelings.

"I was really afraid he wasn't going to wake up, so I began to spill my guts out to him. I held his hand and said how much I loved him and if he would just open his eyes to me, I would love him forever. Suddenly a slight frown come to his face. He snatched his hand from me and said 'Git!' Then he slowly opened his eyes... hurt my feelings." she laughed, and the ladies laughed along with he, "but I was so glad to see him wake up."

"How'd I hurt your feelings" Carson said as he walked into the room catching only the last phrase. "I'm sure I didn't mean to."

"You snatched your hand from me and said 'Git!'" she said.

"Oh," said Carson. "I was still out of it. I thought you were a wolf cub."

"Is that supposed to be funny?" she said as she and the others were preparing to leave.

"No! No, not at all. You have to know the whole story" he explained.

Just then, Ted Dawson came back in. He had been out on the porch talking with Naaman Rum and his sons.

"Are you ready to go?"

"Yes." she answered Ted as the group of visitors were departing.

"I have to talk to my brother," Ted told the group. "He seems to be set on challenging Charley Judson."

"Oh, that's a tall order." Carson responded walking out with them, "I hope he has a changed mind."

"I don't think so." said Ted. "Still, I gotta talk to him."

Dolly was speechless from what she heard, and she wanted to say something but was lost for words.

"Come on and eat something." Mrs. Rum called to Carson. "You can't run off without eating something." So, Carson decided to stay for a while.

As Carson headed inside, the Indians stopped him before they left, "We returned to the Edge at daybreak. Wolves ate outlaw. His gun empty. No bullets in gun belt. Wolves leave head and left hand. We take and burn."

"Yeah, okay. Thanks. Thanks for bringing me here. I guess my horse would have, but I was going so slow, I might not have made it." Carson said shaking their hands.

As soon as Dolly James and Dr. Waller reached Ridgepoint, Dolly went immediately to find Johnny Sweetshot Logan. Upon finding him, she began pleading with him to stop Judson from killing Spud Dawson.

"Dolly," Logan said, "before we came to this town, we had a good thing going. You were a young nurse and there was this deadly gunman named Kane that was out to kill me. Remember? Lucky for me, he took sick. I found out some type of mixture that could relieve him of all pain. You put it in his medicine per my instructions, he drank it down per your instructions. So, I guess I do owe you big time. I'll talk to Top Gun Judson."

"I did tell Kane that stuff would kill him. I guess he thought I was kidding, or like people say, other things will kill you. Either way, I felt like I did my job when I told him."

"Well, I didn't have to live with the fear of him anymore. You came here and landed a new nurse job, I came later and worked on my own gun handling." Logan stated.

As Logan strapped on his two-gun belt, he was thinking. *"Judson isn't going to listen to me. If Spud Dawson goes for him, there'll be no stopping lead from flying. I don't know any other way unless I take on Judson myself."* As he headed for the saloon, he was met by deputy Shelley Weston.

"Johnny," she said with disappointment in her voice, "you promised--you said you'd stay clear of trouble. I see the look in your eyes. You can't tell me you're not up to something."

"Well, yeah, you're right. I am up to something. I'd advise you to leave me alone, Shelley Weston." Sweetshot walked right pass her.

"Johnny, you promised. You must not forget-you're on parole. Johnny, you ARE on parole."

"Jumpin' croppers!" thought Logan. *"She's right."*

"Okay," he turned toward her. "I'll go back to my room and be myself."

As he walked away, he thought, *"I'm gonna have to think of another way to handle this. I can't let Dolly down, even if Dawson has moved her heart. Facing Judson is a tall move I could lose."*

Ted Dawson's trying to convince his twin that he should wait and try to plan out another way. Spud had been practicing his fast-draw and target shooting. The longer he practiced, the angrier he would get. He told his brother that Judson was a gunfighter, and this seemed to excite Dolly. "If she wants a gun fighter," he stated, "that's what I'll be."

"Don't be a fool, Spud" Ted said. "Are you going to challenge a man like Judson?"

"That's where you prove yourself. You think I should start at the bottom?" Spud replied. "If I get him, the rest will respect me."

As Spud checked his gun and started out, Ted made an attempt to stop him. Shelley Weston was walking up in time to see Spud knock Ted to the ground with his gun.

"Sorry, brother but this is something I gotta do," Spud said as he departed.

"Ted! Oh, Ted!" cried Shelley as she helped him from the ground.

As Spud pushed the saloon doors open, he called out for Charley Judson. Joe Bunts ran to Judson's table and told him of Dawson's presence.

"The kid's crazy," said Judson. "He can't out draw me. Go chase yourself Dawson." he said as he rose to his feet. "I got no beef with you."

"Yeah" said Dawson. "Beef! Funny you should say that."

"Look, kid!" said Judson, "This is your last warning."

"Top-Gun, huh?" yelled Spud. "Draw!" and he went for his gun, but Judson was faster. Both guns blazing, Judson dropped Spud to the floor.

When Logan got the news, he was quite disturbed. He knew he would have to console Dolly and offer some kind of reason for not confronting Judson as he told her he would. When Sheriff Steve Wynn investigated, he arrested Judson, but he could not hold him.

"It's only natural that your own henchmen would speak for you," Steve told Judson. "The bar keep was there, Sheriff. He told me to, the man came gunning for me."

When the news hit Gunbelt, Paul Billard decided to ride out near the Edge to make sure his hidden money was not disturbed. When the Sherley brothers heard the news, they decided to check on their stolen money. They missed Paul Billard by fifteen minutes.

Two days later, Kirby Carson and Roy Slim visited the same area. They observed the ragged clothes left by the wolves. They then checked on the stolen loot yet undisturbed.

"Since we're this close to Gunbelt," Carson said to Roy, "let's go have a talk with Billard."

As they rode up to the Sheriff's office in Gun Belt, Rinald Delton sat on the porch in a rocking chair. "Howdy boys" he said as Carson and Roy dismounted.

Billard turned and went back in inviting his visitors to join him. They talked a while and Delton walked in and sat with them. "This isn't private, is it?" he asked.

"Not at all," Carson assured him. "Tell me Paul," Carson said to Billard, "why does Gerry Winson hate you?"

Billard laughed. "I had a couple of run-ins with her brother- down right fist fights. That was before I put on the badge."

"He hooked up with his sister's step-brothers- the Porters. He started with the Sherleys until he found out they were devout enemies," Billard said. "Delton and I are tightening up on the lawlessness of this town. If we could keep the Sherleys away, the Porters are pretty quiet without their uncle."

"Well, every now and then they rattle a few chains," Carson said. "They make sure they are known in all three towns.,"

"After I establish peace, I'm out of here" Billard said. "I've kept Delton here as my deputy just about long enough."

"Yeah" said Delton. "I've gotta get back to Colorado and my family. Most of the criminal element started leaving when Logan got arrested. He had sent for most of them anyway."

"As long as the Sherley boys stay out of our town, the Porter boys are very little trouble" Billard said. "Since King Thompus is not around, they're okay."

"Well, let's ride Roy" Carson said to his deputy. "We will be heading back to Gun-Fire Valley. If you see Bart Winson, you will let us know, won't you?"

"Sure thing, Carson" said Billard. "I see his lovely sister about every day."

As Carson and Roy departed, the three Sherley brothers were riding in. They had seen Bart Winson and felt they had a score to settle with him.

The Sherley brothers split up and went where they thought Bart might be. Mat Sherley headed for Hardy's saloon. Jess March, the Porter's leader, looked out of the saloon door and saw the brother. He frowned when he saw Gus Sherley talking to his daughter Jennifer.

"Hey, Tony," Jess said. "Tell your brothers that trouble is brewing."

"Hey, Louis, the Sherley boys are in town," Tony said.

"Does Mike know it?" Louis asked.

As big Pete Briggs went to the saloon door to stand by his boss, Mat Sherley pushed thru the door.

"Look" he said, "it's Mat Sherley."

"Yeah" Mat said. "What of it?"

"I'm Pete Briggs, that's what!" he said.

"You're a big man Pete. Healthy." Mat said. "Stay out of my way and you'll stay that way."

"If you want trouble" Pete said, "I'm your man."

"Go chase yourself, Briggs," Mat said. "I'm after big steaks."

"I'm a big steak" Pete said, "Get me!"

Grabbing Mat by the shoulder, the fight was on. The two men exchanged some well-placed punches and then big Pete Briggs began to show why he was the three-town champion. He soon proved to be too much for Mat Sherley, he picked Mat up and threw him across a table. Glass went flying like a flock of birds taking off.

Just then, one by one, the other Sherleys came in and joined the fight. One of the Porters asked their boss Jess March if they should help big Pete.

"Sure" said March. "Get in there."

The three Sherley's were putting up a good fight against the Porters. When they realized they could not win, Mat Sherley said, "It's useless boys. Let's gun 'em!"

Drawing their six guns, the gunfight was on. It was a thunderstorm of bullets.

"You're wrecking my saloon!" Jess March shouted as he joined the gun fight. Now nine guns were blasting with men jumping behind tables and whatever obstruction that could provide protection. Curt Sherley caught a deadly slug, Jess March proved to be too big a target, Louis come out shooting because the Sherleys had killed big Pete Briggs, Jess March, Vince and Diken Porter, and both Sherleys shot him as they were backing out of the bar.

The gun battle being over, Tony and Mike Porter stood speechless as they looked down on their fallen brothers and boss in the midst of grey smoke in the air. Bart Winson looked up from an upstairs window of the saloon and watched the two Sherley brothers ride off. He had been sleeping in his hide-away bedroom when the shots rang out.

"That leaves only you and me as the Porter brothers," Tony said to Mike.

"Yeah Mike," Tony answered. "You know man, we'll have to get 'em."

"I'll join you guys' cause," Bart said as he came down the stairs. "I'm with you for as long as it takes."

After the news got around about the gun fight, the townspeople were all the more determined to keep the gunmen on an exodus out of town. They were led by the mayor and council leader Jeff Stacker.

Stacker was working with the mayor to combine the three towns. With towns meetings being held in the three churches, the new church, the town halls, schools, and anywhere the people decided to assemble, it was not long before the gunmen moved on one by one. However, the Porters kept close to the area and the Sherleys stayed away, but not too far away. In Ridgepoint, Charley Judson was keeping quiet as long as no one challenged him. However, that was to be short lived.

The saloon was taken over by Dennis Webb, a gambler called "Three Queens" Denny. Johnny "Sweet Shot" Logan had run two different saloons before being imprisoned. He had no employment since his release, so he set out to get the Hardy's saloon from Dennis Webb. Gambling was his game.

After the funeral of Spud Dawson, a mass funeral was held three days later for Louis, Vince and Diken Porter. Peter Briggs' and Jess March's funerals were held separately. Gus Sherley secretly attended March's funeral so he could see Jennifer March. Little did she realize he was involved in the shootout that killed her father. She didn't know him. With outlaws moving out of the once-lawless towns, the outlaw haven seemed to be no more. Feeling that his job was done, Ronald Delton departed for home in Colorado.

Shortly after, Paul Billard resigned his office as sheriff. Roy Slim was hired to stand in until the town of Gunbelt elected a new sheriff. Billard had an appointed time to leave town. Roy Slim watched him closely and kept Kirby Carson informed.

With Rin Delton gone and Billard no longer wearing a badger, Tony and Mike Porter felt like the law was being diminished, so they told Bart Winson to saddle the horses.

"We're going back to Gunbelt," Tony said. "Mike says it's time. It's still our town. Gerry's been keeping us posted on what's goin on."

Ironically, the Sherley brothers came to town two days later. Mat viewed the town secretly trying to get a lead on the Porters. Gus was taking up time with Jennifer March. Mat spotted Bart Winson, but as he was going after him, he saw Paul Billard making the same approach. As Billard walked upon Winson, Mat stood around the corner of the building and listened. The conversation had already began when he heard Billard say, "I say you know where the Porter boys are?"

"Go away Billard! Leave me alone. I'm not telling you where they are. I will tell people who you are, Mr. Paul Bolton. How long you gonna keep that hid?" Just then Gerry Winson walked up.

"You again!" she said. "You're only trying to get my brother into trouble. If he did know, is it your business? You're not a sheriff anymore."

"Gerry Winson," said Bart to his sister. "You stay out of this. I'm a man! I can handle my affairs."

"Ohhhh, I hate you!" she said to Billard staring at him with fire in her eyes. "If you ever cross me, I'll kill you!"

"Likewise, ma'am!" smirked Billard.

"No" said Bart to Billard, "I'm not telling where the Porters are, and if anybody don't like it, tell 'em to see Bart Winson."

Just then, Mat Sherley stepped from behind the building and said, "Anybody that's pullin' for the Porters is against us Sherleys!" and he shot Bart Winson down. "Don't draw Bolton, or you're as dead as Bart Winson."

"Bart!" cried Gerry as she kept to her brother's side.

"I wouldn't cry too much over him ma'am. Anybody that disagrees with a Sherley is not long for this world."

As Sherley backed away, Gerry Winsons said to Billard, "It's your fault, Mr. Paul Bolton. I'll kill you if it's the last thing I do."

Billard stood silently as Roy Slim came around the corner with his gun drawn.

"Great time o' day!" said Roy looking down at the dead body on the floor.

"He's gone sheriff," Billard said to Roy. "It was Mat Sherley. He killed Bart Winson."

In another part of town, Gus Sherley was walking down the walkway with Jennifer March. Suddenly Mike and Tony Porter began shooting at him. They remembered the gun fight that had taken their brothers. They recalled that the fist fight turned into a gunfight without warning. They were not about to warn Gus Sherley. The first shots missed. Gus pleaded with Jennifer to run--take cover as he drew his gun and fired back. Jennifer refused to leave. Gus was hit. As he fell to the ground the townspeople came running.

As the people watched the Porters ride off, they then turned to Jennifer who was pleading for them to help her get her friend to the doctor. Without question the people assisted the wounded man to a hotel room while one man rode to find a doctor. A horse doctor was found until Dr. Waller could come from Gun-Fire Valley.

———————⌁◇◇⌁———————

While the time for healing went by, the Porters were not seen for a while. Thinking they had killed Gus Sherley, they stayed clear once again from Gunbelt. Mat Sherley eased into town off and on, to check on his brother.

As Jennifer continued to care for Gus Sherley, he decided to let her know who he was. "I think it was my brother Curt that shot your father. It wasn't me," he told her. Of course, she was totally upset in learning the truth of the matter. She had to take some time to let it all sink in. Her friend Helen Linders tried to convince her to give up the man. It was fruitless.

Paul Billard walked into Roy Slim's office and said to him, "Sheriff, I'm just not going to be content until those Porters are behind bars or dead. How about making me your deputy. I was ready to leave town, but then, well, I'm just not satisfied. This last shooting convinced me."

"Fine with me Paul," said Roy. "We can always use help in keeping peace." Roy thought to himself, *"Man it'll be easier now to keep an eye on him."*

As it turned out, Mat Sherley was pinching off the hidden money to pay Gus's doctor and hotel bills. He was returning so often that eventually he had to run into one of the wolves of the Edge Area. He knew he had to be careful. Even worse than that, his final trip found a saddled horse tied to a tree. Sheriff Billard was also pinching off his stolen loot to send to his family. Neither man knew of the other man's hidden money.

As Billard was coming out of the cave, he shot a rattlesnake. Mat hid and watched for Billard to leave. Afterward he ran in, thinking that Billard had found the Sherley money. After checking his loot, he sat for a moment wondering why Billard was there. As Billard walked his horse from the area, his horse whinnied at Sherley's horse, hidden behind a larger boulder. This caused Billard to look curiously around for the horse's rider. Not seeing anyone, he decided to hide and watch to see if anyone would come for the horse.

Shortly after, Mat came and mounted his horse. When Mat rode off, Billard went back to check his money again. It was undisturbed. He then mounted up trying to decide whether or not to chase Mat Sherley. He decided against it. As he reached town, he saw Gerry Winson. He wanted to tell her that he had seen her brother's killer, but he also decided against telling her. She would no doubt ask him why he didn't kill him or something, so he headed for the office of the sheriff. He also decided not to mention it to Roy Slim, or Roy would ask where he saw him.

In Ridgepoint, Mayor Lee Venon Rose was yet trying to romance Dolly James, but his civic duties were keeping him busy. Uniting the three towns was the top of the agenda. Dolly's free time was being taken up by Johnny 'Sweet Shot' Logan. They had such a close connection that it was infuriating Charley Judson.

When a farmer's son charged into the saloon to call Judson's hand, Joe Bunt yelled to Judson, "Turk Haley is comin' for you, Jud!"

"I'm ready. People have to know I do run this town," Judson said.

"Make your play Judson!" called Turk.

"Make yours, Turk," said Judson. Both men bent for leather. Judson was faster. As Turk Haley fell to the floor dead, Judson said to his henchmen, "All right boys, haul him out. He was swift."

Sheriff Steve Wynn took Charley Judson to jail.

"I can't hold him long," he said. "Everyone says Turk drew first."

"I know," said Ted Dawson. "I know." Shortly afterward, the farmer Nate Haley loaded his shotgun to avenge his son.

"He shot Turk, eh?" Nate said. "Turk was my boy. I'm going after the side-winder."

The family tried to stop him, but Nate would not be stopped. Once again it was Joe Bunts that informed Judson. "Old man Nate Haley's coming with a shotgun," Bunt said.

"I'm ready," said Judson. "I'll take on the whole family today."

Before Haley could enter the saloon, Top Gun Judson shot him down. The townspeople were furious. They continued their meetings.

"Since the other outlaws and gunmen left, things seem to be worse. Ever since Rin Delton left, Judson's gone crazy! We've got to get rid of this man," one man stated.

As the meetings continued, Charley Judson's henchmen were keeping him informed on the comments.

"Scared are they?" asked Judson. "If they think I was afraid of Delton, or even Ben Masters, they're crazy!"

"We know," Tom Jacobs said. "We don't want the army coming to wipe us out. We're both tired of hiding and camping out--finding no rest, chased by posse after posse."

"Yeah", said Judson. "When I led the gang in Denver, I was on top, but things got too hot. We ruled, you and I, but the law began picking off the boys one by one. We wore out several horses trying to escape the rope and out necks, sweating thinking about hanging. Then I found this place. Rest at last. No more sleeping on the cold hard ground with tumbleweeds interrupting our sleep."

"So that's why you were so quiet," Jibbs said.

"A man gets tired of running," Judson said.

"Yeah," Jacobs added. "Mighty tired."

"And remember my court trial?" asked Judson. "I told the Judge Haney I have to defend myself even in court. Louis Porter is dead. I speak for myself."

And then Jeff Stacker stated, "How do you know old Nate Hale wasn't trying to sell that shotgun?"

"But Judge Haney is all right," Judson continued to say. "He banged down that gavel and said, 'It's already been established what Haley's intentions were!' Then he declared the case dismissed."

"What about that?" Tonns and Bonds both laughed.

"Yeah boss," Bonds said. "We've got it pretty soft here in Ridgepoint."

"Well, we need to keep it soft, but Stacker is not going to let it rest," Judson said.

⚬ⅢⅢⅢ⚬

A week or more later, Mat Sherley stood across the street from the Gunbelt jail watching for sheriff Roy Slim to leave. After Roy left, Sherley walked in to talk to Paul Billard.

"Easy deputy, I'm not here for trouble," Mat said as he entered the office.

"What do you want, Sherley?" Billard asked

"Just want to talk," said Mat, "let's face it, Billard, you and I have a lot in common."

"What do you mean Sherley? What are you getting at?" Billard asked.

"That cave near the Edge. I've just been burnin' to know why you were there! You weren't hunting rattlers," Mat said.

"Actually," replied Billard, "I was wondering the same thing about you."

"Are you going to satisfy my curiosity?" Mat asked. "I'm taking a huge risk coming here."

"Yeah, I know, and I agree. I know about you, Sherley," Billard said.

"And I know about you, Mr. Paul Bolton! Now let's stop playing games. What about the cave?"

"Well now," said Billard, "since you know who I am, you also know you can't outdraw me. So why are you risking all this just to ask me about the cave?'

"I got the last of my loot out of that cave. I wanted to make sure you weren't skimming off my money." Billard laughed.

"What? You took a chance like you're taking to ask me that? I never even seen your loot."

"Okay Billard," Mat said. "All is well. I-I had to know. I never saw anything you may have hidden in that cave, not to mention I never ever saw another human being in that area except my brothers, I'll be on my way now."

"Not so fast, Sherley," Billard said. "How'd you find out who I was?"

"I'm an outlaw, man. I've always known. "Billard!" Where'd you get a name like that?"

"Careful, Sherley", Billard said. "You're not out the door yet."

"Sure I am" said Mat. "I have an ace!"

"Ace?" asked Billard. "What's your ace?"

"I recovered an old wanted-poster of your brother and you- all dead but you. I put it where Gerry Winson could find it. Nice reward for you too. She'll love that. I walk out of here; I can recover it before she finds it."

"Walk!" said Billard. "Walk!"

The next day, Tony Porter spotted Mat Sherley coming around the building after visiting his brother. He ran swiftly and got his brother Mike. The two Porters waited for Mat to come out of the saloon. As he was about to mount his horse, the Porter brothers began firing on him. As Mat Sherley fell to the ground, the Porters put a rope around his ankles and dragged him through the streets of Gunbelt. After this bizarre display, the Porters, thinking that Gus Sherley had died in the previous shooting, were preparing to show them for the last time in Gunbelt.

"We'll show this town that the Porters have won. They can have their high-minded town! We will survive!"

However, Gus Sherley's landlord saw the house the Porters had entered and informed Gus. Therefore, Gus Sherley checked in his six gun and quietly tip-toed toward the house. Just as the Porters were about to spring to present themselves to the people, Gus Sherley sprang in, firing away. The Porters jumped behind furniture drawing their guns.

"Great guns!" exclaimed Mike. "He must be a ghost! I thought we--we shot him down months ago. Are you hit Tony? Where are you hit, Tony?'" But no answer came from Tony Porter.

"If you're talking to your brother, he's dead," answered Gus Sherley from his hiding place.

"T-Tony!" called Mike. "By gosh, he is dead. I'm coming after you Sherley!"

"Come on" invited Gus. Both men emerged from their furniture forts. Each man fired at the same time. Both men were struck through the heart. The feud between the Porter brothers of the Gunbelt and the Sherley brother from Ridgepoint and beyond was finally ended. With the

Sherley brothers gone, Kirby Carson and Roy Slim could not help but wonder if the stolen money was still there. Upon returning to the cave, the two lawmen found all the money removed. Mat had used most of theirs to take care of his wounded brother and Paul Billard, planning to leave town and rejoin his family had sent the last of his to Indiana. The lamps and candles were gone as well.

After Roy Slim headed back to Gunbelt, he found his deputy's badger lying on his desk on his arrival.

"I'm going on Roy", Billard told him. "I've got a long trip to make. I'm gonna stuff myself with the biggest meal I can hold. That way it'll be a while before I get hungry.

Gerry Winson was settling down to a sizable meal herself. Figuring that she might be arrested for carrying out their plan to shoot down Paul Billard, she decided to eat well while she is free. Feeling she has practiced with her two forty-fours, long enough, she felt ready and bent on revenge still feeling that Billard had caused her brother's death. As Paul Billard was saying goodbye to sheriff Roy Slim, Jennifer March had accompanied her friend Helen Linders who was visiting Roy at his office. As Roy bided Billard goodbye, the ladies were holding Paul Billard in conversation…

This gave Gerry Winson enough time to catch up with Billard. She had found the wanted poster where Mat Sherley had placed it and was killed before he could retrieve it. As Billard said farewell to the two schoolteachers, he heard yet another female voice: "Oh there you are Mr. Billard--or is it Bolton?" It was Gerry Winson, flashing a smile.

"I'm going to get money for doing something I'd love to do. Kill you Mister!"

"Now look sister", Paul said, "I've always had kind of a crush on you, but I really must be going."

"Oh," she said, "you would flirt at such a time as this?"

"Whatever works my dear," Paul answered with a smile. "Whatever works."

"First, I am not your 'dear', and second, time is up," Gerry said. "Are you ready to draw?"

"Well now first of all, if you've never shot a man before, you'd best to aim for the biggest part of him," Paul said, "cause if you miss, you don't get another shot."

"Dead center, Mr. Paul Bolton! Dead center. That's where I'd already planned to hit you...but enough talk."

"Maybe you need to know that I just had a huge meal. I don't think my stomach can hold anything more."

"You're being silly, why don't we find out," she said as she began backing up. "Draw!" She demanded.

Roy Slim had been shuffling paperwork in his office and was paying no attention to what was taking place on the outside.

As Gerry Winson drew her guns, a large belch was heard coming from Paul Billard, interfering with his fast draw. The sound was cut off by the two shots Gerry sent into Billard's belly. Both her shots popped buttons from Billard's shirt.

"Oh!" said the schoolteachers as they ran into each other's arms as they watched Paul Billard hit the ground backward.

"One less outlaw," Gerry said as she blew the smoke from her guns.

Roy Slim came charging out of his office as a crowd was gathering. "Great time o'day!" he exclaimed. After researching his legal paperwork, Roy Slim told the crowd that Billard was an outlaw and he was Paul Bolton-wanted dead or alive.

"Apparently," said Roy, "somebody wanted him dead."

"Don't forget my money dear sheriff," Gerry said to Roy Slim.

"You'll get your reward lady, but maybe you ought to take those six-guns off before they weigh you down about six feet under," Roy said.

As the news reached Ridgepoint about the shooting, Jeff Stacker and the mayor, Lee Venon Rose, were continuing to try to annex the three towns.

"One town is three miles from the other and the other is five miles. New people are settling between the towns. Homesteaders and farmers- we can have one large territory with a degree of respect," Rose said, "but we must push harder to make it a peaceful settlement."

"With Carson, Slim and Wynn, we can combine our law enforcement," Stacker added. "This area has prosperity written all over it. But the bottom line is, we won't be recognized unless we get rid of the lawless gunplay."

When Charley Judson found that the meetings were yet continuing, he said to his men, "Let 'em meet. I'll stop 'em when I'm ready. I'm still determined to run this town."

Three Queens Denny was tending the bar with his bartender when a tall black man wearing two guns walked in and ordered a whiskey stroking his handle bar mustache. The bartender looked at his boss: whether to serve the man or not was the question all over his face.

"Give him drink," Judson said rising from his table. "I'm paying." As the bartender nervously poured the drink, Judson walked over to the bar.

"We don't generally serve his kind," Denny said to Judson. "Never!"

"His kind?" Judson asked.

"Him, his kind, and Injuns!" Denny said.

"You'll serve him," Judson said. "I've been wanting to talk to him."

"I can pay," the man stated.

"I'm sure of that," said Judson, "but let me."

"You say you wanted to talk to me huh? Then why didn't you come to the church? I'm sure that's where you saw me."

"That's right. Guarding the church. I've always wondered why. Why would you have to guard a church?" Judson asked. "You people expected trouble?"

"I've traveled with the preacher over various areas for ome time. We've had more trouble from sagebrush and tumbleweeds than from people. Once they see my guns, they figure I can use 'em."

"Yeah, I figured as much. The way you wear 'em; the way they hang just right, yeah, I'm sure you can use 'em," Judson said. "Matter of fact, I know you can."

"You know huh?" the man asked.

"I know," said Judson. "I've seen you before."

"There was a battle going on with the cavalry and Indians," Judson continued. "I remember you and some more of your group fighting on the side of the cavalry."

"Sure," said the man, "we were in the cavalry."

"Yeah, I know," said Judson, "but after the battle, the Indians were askin' why you were on the side of the white man."

"Yeah," said the man, "I recall. They had a good question. We've never been able to answer that." The man started to walk out when Judson said, "One more question. If you're such a church man, why are you drinkin' whiskey?'

"It's to steady my nerves. Sometimes my gun hand gets a little excited when people ask too many questions. Thanks for the drink." The man said and he walked out. The he turned and said, "I'm not a saint yet. I still have a couple more vices to overcome."

At that, the man mounted his horse and rode away.

"Wow," said Squint, "That was salty. I wanted to take him."

"No, you didn't," said Judson. "Not that guy. No, you didn't!"

"You seem to know him," said Toby, "what's his name?"

"His name is Brian Elliott Carter McClure," Judson answered.

"Okay," said Toby. "Okay, I had to ask."

"That's some name," Squint said.

"Yeah, a long name," said Rory.

"His conquests are just as long as his name," Judson said. "Quite a man. I wanted to tell him that as ruthless as some men are, we wouldn't hardly bother a church. That would be too salty. Too overboard."

Two days later, Charley Judson sent Joe Bunts to find Dolly James. She was just leaving Dr. Waller's office. As she walked into the saloon, he called her over. "Give us room boys," he told his henchmen. As the men walked away, Judson asked Dolly to sit down. He placed a small stack of bills on the table. Bills- ten one-hundred-dollar bills.

"Take it, honey. It's yours," he said. Dolly looked at him and then she said, "I haven't done anything to earn that."

"I know. Take it. I said it's yours." He slid the bills over to her.

"You know you can't buy love, Charley. Why would you try?" she asked and slid it back.

"I feel like it's worth a try. I'm smart enough to know a guy can't buy love. If I decide to try anyway, I'm willing to give up a grand. I have lost more than that gambling. I do insist. Now take it."

Dolly folded her arms. "Oh Charley, this is ridiculous. I've got to go back. I don't have time to argue about this. You know, I can always use the money. Why would you tempt me this way?"

"Go ahead, take the dough. If I lose, I lose. At least you might think of me while spending it."

"Well," she said as she picked up the money, "I won't promise that, but thank you Charley."

As Charley Judson watched her walk away, he ordered a bottle of whiskey and said to his men; "Leave me be boys. I'm gonna drown myself in whiskey. Maybe I make more sense drunk. Hey, I'll be counting every heartbeat she takes with every dollar she spends."

Toby looked at Squint as they watched Judson turn up the whiskey bottle.

"That was hot money," Judson said. "I probably wouldn't have won it all from Denny if he wasn't so scared of me." Then he laughed and downed more whiskey right from the bottle.

"The boss is losing it," said Rory Jibbs to Tom Jacobs. He gave that whole stack to Doll-face. You ever seen something like before in all your life?"

"Yep," said Jacobs. "I've seen it. I lived it. It was a dancehall in Denver. She was a fine dancehall gal. I had my cut from a bank robbery. She laughed when I gave it to her. She knew I'd never see her again. I guess ol' Charley got it from me- giving away that dough."

"A whole grand?" asked Rory- "That's a lot of cheddar! How did you--I mean, what'd you do about it?"

"I robbed another bank and got drunk," Jacobs said.

"You think the boss will rob a bank?" Joe Bunts asked.

"He might do something just as crazy," Jacobs answered.

The next evening, Charley Judson waited for the town meeting. As Jeff Stacker and Lee Venon Rose was addressing the crowd, Stacker stood and called on each man that wanted to speak. One man said, "We have to go to other towns sometimes to shop. We don't want to see Judson or any of his men." Another man was speaking as Steve Wynn walked in.

"Even our sheriff, the great Steven Wynn himself, an old gun man, seems helpless towards Charley Judson." The man felt embarrassed as Wynn came in.

"Well," said another, "his deputy, whose own brother fell by Judson's guns, fails to fight." Just then, Ted Dawson and Shelley Weston walked in.

"We must decide to stick together," Lee Venon Rose spoke up. "This committee is to decide what to do something about this gunfighter."

"It'll be tough," another man said. "For three or so months there's been no killings or any such crime in this town. Some of us were wondering if Judson was still around. Then we found out that he was."

Standing outside, Charley took a drink of whiskey from his bottle and walked in. Jeff Stacker had the floor. He was waving his fist in the air and saying, "--so we must all do our part to protect this town. We have a chance to expand our territory. So, I say run Judson out!"

"Those were brave words Stacker!" Judson said as he walked in. "Now, back 'em up!"

"J-Judson!" said Stacker. "N-now wait, Judson! I-I'm not a gunman. I wasn't the only one."

"Draw Stacker!" Judson demanded.

"Hold it Judson, in the name of the law!" Steve Wynn said as he drew his gun. Judson's men entered.

"I said draw Stacker or die anyway!"

Judson took a step back and drew both his guns. He shot Steve in the right shoulder causing him to drop his gun. He fired a shot into Stacker and held his guns on Ted.

"How about it, deputy?" Dawson held his hands up. Judson laughed and said, "What's the matter Dawson?" Judson's men watched with guns out.

"Haven't you done enough already, Charley Judson?" asked Shelley.

"Well, well, well," Judson said. "The women taking up for the men!" He laughed and said, "that beats it all! Okay lovely, if you say so, I'll go."

As Judson backed out with both his guns yet drawn, Shelley went to Steve's side.

"We'll get 'em," said Dawson. "I swear it!"

"I'll get him for old and new!"

"How is Stacker?" asked the sheriff as he clutched his wounded shoulder.

"We think he might make it. Time will tell," the horse doctor said. "Hurry, somebody get Doc Waller here!"

In another building, Johnny Sweetshot Logan had heard the shots. As Dolly James walked into the room he asked: "Doll-face, what was that shooting about?"

"How should I know?" she answered.

"I'm going to see," he said. "If it's that Judson guy, I'll-"

"No," she said, "I won't let you!"

"Wha-a-at?" he said. "Are you still stuck on that guy?"

"Oh, stop it Sweet Shot," she said. "That's the same thing---" then she stopped.

"What were you going to say, Doll-face?" he asked.

"Nothing," she said. "Well, that's the last thing Spud had said before he went after Charley."

"You think I'm not fast enough, maybe?" he asked.

"Maybe," she said.

"Okay," he said. "I can take a hint. Well, maybe I have slowed up a bit. Okay. I can practice some more and if Charley Judson ever crosses me, he will regret it."

"Are you sure?" she asked.

"Don't push me, Doll-face. I just might go and get him now!" Logan stated.

"No, darling," she said. "Don't."

After Dr. Waller patched up the wounded men, he told the sheriff that he would have to take it easy for a while. Jeff Stacker almost died from a high chest wound, but he was strong enough to pull through. The preachers from the three churches were there at the meeting. They prayed over Stacker, and he was able to survive.

Ted Dawson told sheriff Wynn that it was his duty to go after Charley Judson. The sheriff told him that he would have to wait. The time was not right. Ted declared he was going anyway. The sheriff ordered him not to go. Shelley Weston pleaded with Ted to listen to the sheriff and wait. The sheriff had to threaten to fire Ted as a deputy if he would disobey orders.

"A man can't hide it when he's scared," Steve said. "I can't nor can any other man in this town. I'm supposed to be their leader, and I can't hide it. We will wait. Something will break. It always does."

The fourth of July rolled around a week later. The festivities took place with Kirby Carson riding Cony and Shelley Weston riding Midnight. Roy Slim rode Dust, and Chief Flaming Eagle rode Nightwind. The race was close and exciting. Once again, it was Midnight as the winner. Flaming Eagle was second riding Night Wind with Carson a close third. Roy Slim felt that Carson could have been second.

"You could've beat the chief," Roy said to Carson. "Well, I guess we'll never know, will we?" Carson said to Roy.

The boxing and wrestling took place without Carson.

"We have to set up a new champ since Briggs is gone. Curt Sherley was leading contender after Carson, but he's no more. The winner of the next matches will meet Carson for the title," Mayor Lee V. Rose stated.

Bold Arrow, one of Chief Flaming Eagle's braves, was among the contenders for wrestling. While the festivities took place, Charley Judson was laying low. His men began to question his bravery.

"You're not going to the festival grounds? We usually go, you know," Squint said to Judson.

"These people don't want to see me or any of my men," Judson said. "You can go if you want to."

"You haven't caused any trouble since you shot the sheriff," Squint said. "People will think that scared you into slowing it down."

"What do you think Squint?" Judson asked.

"Me?" answered Squint, "I know better. I know what's what!"

Suddenly a stranger walked in saying, "Well, I Don't! Get ready, Judson!"

"He's busy," said Jacobs. "Try me, Mister."

"I'm not after you Tom," the stranger said.

"How'd you know me? Huh?" Tom Jacobs asked.

"Like I said," said Judson, "he was tricky! Shifty! Quick on the draw!"

"Why was he after you, Boss, and how did he know each of us? Joe asked.

"I fell in love with his girlfriend. She despised me. I choked her to death--I guess I didn't really mean to kill her---well, anyway, he came here looking for me, he learned you guys from your gambling while checkin' each man. He knew Tom from Denver.

"Yeah," said Tom Jacobs, "I thought I knew him from somewhere--but isn't he--isn't he--"

"Yeah, Tom," Judson said. "He was my brother!"

"Your brother?" asked Joe.

"My half-brother- James Judson. He didn't recognize my new look when he was here before- before the townspeople even knew who I was. Once he found that I was here, he headed back to get me."

"That's heavy, Charley," Tom said.

"Let's have a drink and then we'll put him in the ground," Judson said. "At this point, I'm sick of Killin! The next guy that challenges me, you guys can have him."

They then took the body away.

As Charley Judson walked up the saloon stairs up to his room with a whiskey bottle, his henchmen sat at their regular gambling table and began a game.

"You know," said Jacobs to the men, "Charley and me- we go a long way back. I have never seen him…"

"So stressed out. He's drinking more, he--well look! He wounded Stacker and Wynn. He never just wounds a man. Not Charley."

"What are you getting at Tom?" Rory asked.

"Look! He's changed. 'Tired of killing' he said. I think it's the girl. He's lost his head over Dolly. He won't admit it. Look at the loot he whipped on her--for nothing. The most he ever got from her was a hug! Not even a kiss! A hug, I tell ya!"

"Well, you said you threw a grand on that dancehall girl for nothing," Squint added.

"Yeah, but I robbed the same bank she dealt with. I got mine back," Tom said, "of course, it didn't have to pan out that way, anyway, I didn't go to drinkin' more- I didn't drink less, but I didn' drink more like he's doing. Besides, I did like that dance hall girl. Had we hung around there, I would have gotten to her, but Charley's letting Dolly go."

"I guess he realized Logan and Rose have a better grip on her," Rory stated.

"Knowin' that, why still try to buy her--" Tom continued. "Well, okay. I'm lettin' it go, but I'm still a little worried about my buddy."

Sheriff Steve Wynn is yet concerned about the recent shooting of James Judson, but still recovering from his shoulder wound, he continued to stay clear. The townspeople were aware of the incident, but they kept silent as well. The sheriff knew he couldn't do too much with his left hand and he defied his deputies to do anything without him.

After a week of quietness, Cole, the hardware owner, was shot by Rory Jibbs. Deputy Ted Dawson, upon hearing the shots, ran quickly to see what the shots were about. After learning it was Jibbs, he declared "I'll get him!"

Before Jibbs could get back to the safety of the saloon, Ted caught up with him, "you're under arrest Jibbs!"

"Yeah?" said Jibbs, "try and take me Deputy Ted Dawson!" and he backed into the saloon drawing his gun. Ted fired, killing Rory Jibbs. Judson dropped a cigarette from his mouth, Squint dropped his whiskey bottle, and the others prepared to reach for their guns, but Ted's six gun was already drawn on them. Jibbs had laughed and said, "you're scared to take me, I know! I'm Rory, one of Judson's men. Now speak your bold talk!"

Once again, Ted told him he was under arrest, then the shooting of Rory Jibbs, "Gun him down," Tom shouted.

"First one to draw gets drilled!" Dawson said.

"Hold it Tom," Judson said.

"You can't get all five of us," Judson said, "and we'll get you before you reach the door!"

"You can get me," Ted said, "but I'll get one of you, and believe me, you'll feel it. If I go down, I'll go down doing my duty."

Just then, the saloon doors swung open and in stepped Johnny 'Sweetshot' Logan with guns drawn. "I'm on Dawson's side," he said. "Draw and you're dead."

"Sweetshot Logan," Judson said. "This your last time meddlin'!"

"If you want me, I'll be back," Logan said, "and my guns will be holstered. Let's go Dawson."

"Good." said Judson.

As Logan and Dawson departed, Judson said, "they're going to the sheriff's office. You boys go after them. Gun 'em down!"

"You comin', Boss?" Joe asked.

"I've got a score to settle with Doll-face. When you get back, you'll each get a grand. Now git!"

As the men mounted up, Tom said: "I told you he changed. He's got that girl on his mind."

"You think we can take these guys?" Joe asked.

"Well, there's a crippled sheriff. What can he hit with a left hand? You'd better go for him Joe. Then there's Logan. Who knows how he got that nickname. Maybe Squint should go for him. Now Dawson? -- and the girl? Which do I want?" Tom pondered.

"Maybe I want the girl," said Toby. "I've had fantasy dreams about facing her in a gunfight."

"You guys better make up your minds," said Squint. "We're here."

As Ted looked out of the jail, he said, "They're here. Seems they've after me for killin' Jibbs."

"I can be of little help left-handed," Steve said.

"Well, I can help," Shelley said. Then turning to Johnny Logan

"It's two to four. Logan? Oh please, Johnny."

"All right sheriff," Logan said. "How about deputizing me."

"I have no choice. Welcome Logan," Steve said as he gave Logan a quick oath.

As they stepped out of the jail to meet Judson's men, the men spread as they reached for their guns.

"Drop your guns!" Steve shouted as he took his gun in his left hand. Judson's men were so unorganized without him, they just drew their guns and started to shoot. They were still disputing on which lawman to shoot.

Logan wounded Squint, Dawson wounded Toby Bonds, and Shelley sent two slugs into Tom Jacob's belly. Joe Bunts ran as fast as he could looking for Charley Judson.

"He'll be looking for Judson," Logan said. "I'd better see if he's at Dolly's. Take care of these two."

As Charley Judson knocked on Dolly's door, she said "Come in Sweetshot."

"Maybe I do shoot sweetly, but I'm not Johnny Logan."

"Charley," she said, "what are you doing here?"

"I came to kill you Dolly," he said.

"What?" Dolly' face went from curious to shock. "But why?"

"Why, you ask," he said, "I think I kinda ran out of something to do."

Joe Bunt's voice was heard outside Dolly's upstairs window. He was calling for Judson. Judson picked up a liquor bottle that Dolly had.

"Someone's calling you," she said as she slipped to her drawer and grabbed her gun. Judson took a drink.

"It's Joe Bunts," he said as he opened the window.

"What is it, Joe?" he said as he took another drink.

"Huh? Oh, there you are. What'cha doing up there? Come here," Joe called.

"Come down? Why Joe? What happened?"

As Joe began to tell Judson how the gun battle ended, Judson spotted Logan coming down the back alley.

"Hey, Joe, hide. Logan is coming. You can gun him as he walks by," Judson said. "I'll get him from up here."

During this time, Steve was looking for Logan. "I've got this copy of his release paper. Ted, how about taking this to him," Steve said. But Ted and Shelley were being romantic and making wedding plans.

"Oh, all right," Steve said, "I'll take it myself."

As Logan was approaching Dolly's building, Bunts was hiding behind the barrow. As Judson waited at the upstairs window, Dolly put her gun in his back.

"Drop the gun, Charley, or I'll shoot," she said.

"You wouldn't dare," he said.

"Oh? And why wouldn't I?"

"If you shoot me, Logan will get it in the back. He'll hear a shot and think Joe is up here. He's probably looking for him anyway. So why don't you go ahead and draw his attention."

"Oh!" she said. "Oh!"

"You may as well give me your gun baby," he said as he turned and snatched the gun from her hand. "And also, if you yell or scream, you'll make it easy for Joe to gun him."

Dolly began easing toward the door. Judson turned again from the window and ran to grab her.

"I came to kill you, Doll face. You cost me a grand just to fall for two other men. I didn't do anything because nobody even knew me around here. Now that I'm known, it doesn't matter."

"If-if I don't scream, you'll kill Johnny," she said.

"I won't even draw my gun unless Joe misses," he said. As Bunts rose up from hiding and aimed his gun at Logan, Steve came around the corner. "It's Joe--he's going to-- not if I can help it."

"Drop it Joe!" Steve shouted. "Or I'll shoot! We're the law! We have to rise to the challenge!"

"You're too late, Wynn!" Joe said. "He's as good as dead." As Joe fired, he barely missed.

"Jumpin' croppers!" exclaimed Logan.

"Nervousness took you, Joe. You won't get another shot!" Steve's left-handed shot hit Joe in the back of his head. "Not bad for a left-handed shot," Steve said.

"Wow," said Logan, "Thanks Steve. Thanks a lot. That was some shot! That was too close!"

"Yeah," said Steve. "We've been really lucky this day. That shooting outside the office and now this."

In Dolly's apartment, Charley Judson was boiling with anger.

"Everyone meddles in this town. A man can't even kill a guy unless--"

"Charley listen," Dolly said. "You don't have to kill me. You don't want to anyway."

"Maybe not, Doll-face Dolly," he said. "Maybe not--but I do want to kill Logan, and I'm sure you would try to stop me, so I might as well kill you both."

"Look," she said as she ran to the window," he's leaving with the sheriff. You don't have to kill either of us now!"

"Yeah," he thought, "maybe not. Not today. My men--my men are gone. Tom—Tom and I--we go way back."

"Sure," said she, "sure honey! Here, let me get you your money--"

"Money?" he said. "Money--I don't' want that money Doll-face. I want whiskey!" With this, he stormed out of the room, down the steps and out the door.

"Poor tortured soul," she thought as she watched him stagger through the alley. "Oh, my! He took my bottle and he's looking for more."

As Logan and sheriff Wynn arrived at the jail, the undertaker had taken away the body of Tom Jacobs.

Dr. Waller and the town's horse doctor were taking care of Squint Tonns and Toby Bonds as the deputies stood guard. As the deputies, Ted and Shelley awaited, Ted asked Shelley if she was okay after killing her first man.

"I-I was always told that if you really had to kill someone, you must not dwell on it afterward. I knew when I accepted this job of deputy that in a lawless town such as this one is, a day like this would come." she said.

"That's right," Ted said. "It's you or the other guy. I got a good shot off and so did Logan. Our oppositions were lucky. They could've been hauled away by the undertaker as well."

"I had heard what Gerry Winson said about if you were going to shoot a person. Golly! I guess Billard even told her himself. She was telling a group in the saloon what had happened. I was passing thru and heard her. I figured it was well worth remembering," Shelley said.

"Gerry Winson," said Ted. "Yeah, I noticed her at the shooting range on the fourth. She is good. Billard never should've tried her."

"What are you doing noticing her?" Shelley snapped.

"Okay," Dr. Waller said, "these men will have to be hospitalized for a while before they can face jail time. I'll make the arrangements to get 'em there."

Roy Slim rode into Gun-Fire Valley to see his pal Kirby Carson. The news had gotten to all the areas concerning the latest shootings.

"Hey Kirb," Roy said as he rushed into the office. I have got a big problem here."

"What is it, Roy?" asked Carson.

"Look at these papers! Look at this mail--the one marked sheriff Billard. Look at it!" Roy said anxiously.

"Holy smoke!" Carson exclaimed as he looked at the documents.

"Yeah," said Roy, "holy smoke is right!"

The papers and documents for Sheriff Paul Billard, alias Paul Bolton, because he and Rinald Delton had cleaned up the town of Gunbelt, they both received full pardons from the governor. Delton had received his mail in Colorado. Paul Billard received his mail two days before he had faced Gerry Winson's guns. Billard was one of those people who never check their mail for a few days.

"Well," Roy said. "What do you think?"

"He should have checked his mail," Carson said.

"That's only part of it man," Roy said. "I receiver her reward money a few days later and gave it to her."

"Yeah?" asked Carson.

"Look Kirby! You don't get it! Look at the whole picture. Gerry Winson killed an innocent man. Great time o'day!"

"Hmmm" thought Carson.

"I gave her the money! I just happen to be going through paper and mail and 'pow'! There it was," Roy said. "What'll I tell her? Do I arrest her?"

"Well-l-l," said Carson, "he wasn't unarmed. Did he draw?"

"He was defending himself! She challenged him!" Roy said. "...and now--now..."

"Have you seen her lately?" Carson asked.

"Yeah, I've seen her. The gamblers and saloon owners are treating her like a queen. They get the idea they can open up the town again. Shoot 'em up! Billiard is gone! Delton is gone! We can cut loose! Go hog-wild! Bands is dead! What's next?"

"You worried, Roy?" asked Carson.

"Worried? I could use some deputies, but that's not what's before me now," said Roy. "That girl still hates lawmen."

"Worried?" Carson asked again.

"About her? Well-l-l-l maybe. I'm the one who has to tell her. The man got pardoned two days earlier," Roy said. "You killed a pardoned man; I must tell her."

"You know," Roy continued, "if Rin Delton hadn't sent a congratulatory letter to Billard, I might not have checked Billard's mail at all," Roy said. "So Kirb- how do I handle it?"

"Well Roy," Carson said, "you're the sheriff of Gunbelt- handle it!"

"Kirby, are you sore because I left Gun-Fire Valley to take this job?" Roy asked.

"Nonsense," Carson said. "You know I was glad to see you land that job. You're a good lawman."

"Well thanks, "Roy said, "but I still have a problem."

"I'll tell you what," Carson said. "You make me your deputy for Gunbelt and you can still be my deputy here. "We'll both be sheriff and deputy."

"That sounds like a winner," Roy said. "It will make the wild side of town think twice, but I still have to face the girl."

"After I make my rounds, we'll head for your town," Carson said, "and maybe I'll even talk to the girl."

"No, no," Roy said. "I wouldn't put that off on you."

"It's no problem at all," Carson said. "You know I love talking to the ladies."

"Yeah, but Gerry Winson!" Roy said. "How smooth is that going to be."

"I'll chance it Roy," Carson said. "Don't sweat it."

"You know she's King Thompus' niece, don't you?" Roy asked.

"A stepdaughter or something, I guess," Kirby said. "No matter."

Kirby Carson and Roy Slim rode to Ridgepoint to inform Mayor Lee Venon Rose of their collaboration. Rose considered it a splendid move that worked right in with his plan to consolidate the three towns. They then went to see Sheriff Steve Wynn. Carson was not happy to see Shelley Weston with Ted Dawson. They were both deputies, so they were at the sheriff's office as well. Carson congratulated the lawmen for ridding the town of Judson's henchmen.

"I'm glad to see your wounds healed, Kirby. I guess you're back in the saddle," Shelley said.

"Well, Roy, let's ride." As they mounted up and were riding away, Roy looked at Carson and said:

"It's not easy, is it? I know how you feel about her." Carson didn't answer. They rode on toward Gunbelt.

"You know, I've been talkin' time with Helen Linders you know, the schoolteacher, you know?" Roy said. Carson was still silent. Roy continued, "she said Jennifer, her friend, Jennifer March had eyes for you."

"Yeah? Really?" Carson perked up and asked, "she--uh, was pretty stuck on Gus Sherley, wasn't she?"

"She was," Roy said. "She liked him a lot. But you know, he's gone. He's dead. She's alive. You're alive. She likes you man."

Carson laughed. He smiled and laughed again; Roy laughed with him.

"Yeah pal, she likes you buddy."

"Well," said Carson, "she is a fabulous glamorous woman-"

"So, you have noticed her?" said Roy. "Why does that surprise me?" Then they both laughed.

As Roy headed for his office, Carson headed for the saloon. As he entered the saloon, he was amazed to be met at the door by 'Three-Queens' Denny.

"Hey Mr. Webb- 'Three Queens' Denny," Carson said.

"Hello Sheriff," Denny said, "what brings you to our town?

"Just visiting." Carson said. "I'd heard how the men that a lot of gambling goes to each town to each saloon, but you--you run the saloon in Ridgepoint."

"I own 'em both, Sheriff. I have to keep a check on the one in Gunbelt as well as this one. Come on over to the bar. I'm buyin," Denny said.

"Thanks Denny," Carson said. "I accept."

"You know, sheriff, with the cattlemen getting paid one week and the sheep men the following week, they love to gamble. It keeps me jumping to keep it all on the upswing. Charley Judson brought his men in here a few weeks back. I had invited them to come and check out my other saloon. That's the day this two-gunned black man came in. I wasn't gonna serve him. I'm glad I did. He turned out to be famous."

"The church guard huh? I heard about him," said Carson. "Well, Judson's men won't be back, at least three of 'em."

"You know sheriff, he never gave me any trouble," Denny said.

"They'd sit and drink, gamble and drink, then they'd go home and come back the next day. They were good for business."

"Yeah," Carson said. "I guess that depends on what side of the street you're on. Thanks for the drink."

As Carson was walking out, Denny walked with him. "You have to admit, sheriff," he said, "these kinds of men keep us both in business."

"I guess you're right, Mr. Webb," Carson said, "I guess you're right."

Mounting Coney and then turning him around, Carson asked Denny as he was heading back inside: "By the way, Denny, has Gerry Winson been around?"

"Yeah," Denny said. "She was in here on my last trip- The guys were joking about the buttons from Billard's shirt she shot off."

"I guess that was some kind of shootin'," Carson said, and he turned and rode off.

The next day, Johnny Logan walked into the saloon in Ridgepoint to talk to Denny, the owner. As the two sat down in Denny's office, Logan said, "Listen, I am not prying into your business, but I'm curious. I made a good living running this saloon. I also ran the other one in Gun-Fire Valley. What I'm saying is I've been watching you since I returned. You are making more money than I ever did. How about sharing your method with me?"

"I owe the plan to gather the profits to none other than King Thompus the Hat." He said, "if I got a cover charge from every man that wanted to gamble, it could pay pretty good."

"Well! Pay pretty good indeed! Every weekend I need extra help serving customers, extra guards, counting and recounting the dough, hey, both banks are glad to see me coming."

"Alright! Alright!" Logan said, "but—but, also you play a good hand at gambling yourself, Three Queens" Denny. We gamblers know each other, you know. At Gun-Fire Valley, my method wasn't as good."

"Yeah," Denny said. "We all have our own little secrets, don't we? Our own little methods when it's time to rack in the winnings."

"It's more of the house must always win rather than a game of chance," Logan said.

"Hey, I've got so lose some in order to keep 'em coming back. You know that. But I've got a rule, when they pay their house-charge, I tell them to make sure you have taken care of your home duties before you come here to gamble," Denny stated.

"That way, they figure you're a fair man." Logan said. "You cover all the bases."

In another part of town, Mayor Lee Venon Rose was visiting Jeff Stacker as he is recuperating at his home. Nurse Dolly James was checking on Dr. Waller's patient as the mayor walked in. Rose was gladder to see Dolly than he was to see Stacker. As the three sat and talked, Rose let Stacker know of the progress that was being made to annex the properties between the three towns. As people were moving west from the east and middle-west, the areas were becoming settled even faster than the mayor had expected. Blacks, Chinese, other Indians, some Mexicans, along with the usual number of white farmers and homesteaders caused the territory to expand. Some of the newcomers were doctors, blacksmiths, carpenters, and men with other crafts. New life in a new area was what they were looking for.

As well, there were men anxious to see the people who had shot down the dreaded outlaws like Tom Jacobs, Paul Bolton (Billiard) and the places where the Sherleys and Porters had shot it out. The Newsletter, the only newspaper between the three towns had spread the events of each occurrence and bigger newspapers were spreading the messages in other towns and cities. This stirred the heart of some young gunmen that thought maybe they might want to come to the area and consider challenging the guns of Thompus towns.

———

Meanwhile, Roy Slim was waiting to see how Kirby Carson was going to handle the problem at hand with the Gerry Winson incident.

Roy presented the papers and documents to her. "What-what's this?" she asked. "What does this mean?"

"Well ma'am," Roy replied, "what do you make of it?"

"Is this what Carson wanted to show me?" she asked, as she looked the papers over and over. "I'm afraid so, ma'am," Roy replied.

"Will you stop calling me 'ma'am'?!" What are you going to do about this? He was an outlaw! He should have read his mail. I didn't know--you didn't know there was a reward on him. What does Carson have to do with it? Is he pushing you to do something against me? What sheriff?"

"Well now give me a chance to answer ma'am- I mean 'miss'," Roy said. "Great time o'day!"

"Well, where is he if he's your deputy?!"

"He's still sheriff of Gun-Fire Valley. He and I have to pull double-duty," Roy said. "I'm still his deputy."

"You know I don't like him, don't you? I mean, he seem so sure of himself. I'd like to do him the way I did Billard. I guess I just hate lawmen- well, you're some different. I can tolerate you, but Billard--and Carson, well--"

"Okay, Miss" Roy said. "I'm gonna just let it all go until I hear from the governor or even Judge Haney. This is well deep!"

"Well, I'm telling you now sheriff, I am not going to jail. For this? No sir! I'll run first!" Gerry said. At this she walked out.

"Hey," called Roy, "keep your eyes open. I've already got word that some proud guns with nothing better to do may be heading this way to see the gal that outdrew Billard."

"Thanks, badge carrier," she said. "I'm not boasting or anything, and neither do I mean any of this to happen, but if they insist, I'll be ready." Then she rode away.

As she went to her apartment, Gerry began to ponder. "*I like this place. I'm not going to run. If the law wants me, perhaps I can hide in plain sight. As a little girl, I was good at dressing up and becoming someone else. With these new people coming in, I can wear a wig, or change my hair, and get a schoolteacher's job. The boarding house across from the jail in Gun-Fire Valley is a nice second home. As a new person, I can even size up the new guns that might be seeking me.*"

So, this she did. Hiding her blonde hair under a dark brown wig and donning a pair of clear glasses, Gerry Winson became Chryell Ann

Alexander. Mingling with the newcomers that rolled into town in droves, she applied and received a schoolteacher's job for it was much needed with all the new people arriving. Gerry visited her uncle Ex-King Thompus in the territorial prison and disclosed to him all that had transpired.

To be continued....

Printed in the United States
by Baker & Taylor Publisher Services